Randal thought he wanted to be a wizard. . . .

Just before noon, Randal found Madoc in the tower. The wizard was reading a small, leather-bound book.

"What is it, lad?" asked Madoc, not looking up.

"I—I want to be a wizard like you," Randal told him.

"How can you want to be a wizard, boy? You haven't got the foggiest idea of what it's all about." Madoc rose and stood glaring down at Randal. "You'll spend most of your life with just enough power to get you into trouble. You'll be hungry more often than you're fed. You'll spend more time in danger on the road than safe under a roof. And maybe you'll survive it all and live to be old and white-bearded and wise—but if you do, most of your friends will have died a long time before. Go back downstairs to your uncle, lad, and one day you'll make a fine knight. Wizardry is no life for you."

Randal went, but he felt restless and uneasy. Even if wizardry was as hard as Madoc said, it was still the only thing he wanted.

CIRCLE OF MAGIC

SCHOOL OF WIZARDRY

Debra Doyle and James D. Macdonald
illustrated by Judith Mitchell

To Margaret Esterl and W. Douglas Macdonald,
and in memory of Dr. Douglas Amos Paine

This edition published in 2002.

Cover photography by Steven Dolce.

Printed in Canada.

10 9 8 7

I.

A Visitor at Castle Doun

"I TOLD YOU it was going to rain," said Randal. He frowned at the drops spotting the dusty flagstones of the courtyard of Castle Doun. In a minute or two, a layer of slick mud would be covering the pavement.

"And I told you Sir Palamon would have us out here anyway," said his cousin Walter as he strode off toward the pells—thick, man-high poles of wood, notched and chipped from taking sword blows from Castle Doun's knights and squires.

Walter was sixteen and already wearing metal armor. Randal, at twelve and a bit, still practiced in padded cloth and leather. He watched his cousin cutting high and low, left and right, at the pells, and wondered if armor made a difference.

The sound of spurs clinking on the pavement made him turn around. Sir Palamon, master-at-arms for Castle Doun, stood with his thumbs hooked into his belt. "Good to see you boys out here," he said. "Carry on with your practice."

Randal gripped his sword. Again and again he

swung the heavy blade above his head, snapped it forward past his shoulder, and thrust with all his weight behind it. Sir Palamon's hoarse voice interrupted him in mid-motion. "Let's see that last move again—and this time step forward into it!"

Randal thrust with the sword.

Sir Palamon looked disgusted. "What do you think you're doing—poking holes in a sack of flour? Do it again."

Randal tried again. Sir Palamon shook his head and drew his own sword.

"The day may come," said the master-at-arms, "when you won't have your shield, and you won't have your armor, and you won't have your friends beside you—but you'll have your sword and your skill. Those will always be with you. Now watch."

The master-at-arms swung his blade as if cutting at an enemy's leg. At the last moment, he straightened his arm and stepped forward with his rear foot, turning the thrust into a deadly lunge.

"Like that," said Palamon. "Aim for a spot somewhere beyond the other man's back. Now you try."

Randal hefted his sword. Frowning, he tried to see an enemy standing in front of him—no taller than this, no farther than that. He could see where his blow would have to end up, on the other side of the imaginary figure; he thrust and put the sword point there.

"That's more like it," said Palamon. "Keep practicing and don't let your mind wander, and we'll make a knight of you yet."

A shout came from the castle gate. "Stranger coming up the road!"

The wind gusted harder, making the rain sting against Randal's face. "All right, lads," he heard Palamon saying as he headed toward the gate. "The weather's turning nasty—in you go."

Randal took his time getting out of the quilted practice armor; he wanted to see who was coming just as much as Sir Palamon did. These days, with no true king in the land and the great nobles fighting for power, not many people traveled the roads alone.

The newcomer wasn't much to look at: a man about forty years old with a short dark beard, carrying a walking staff taller than he was. He wore a loose shirt of faded yellow linen and a rough kilt of gray wool, belted around his waist and folded up over one shoulder. *He's a long way from home,* thought Randal. Only the half-civilized tribesmen of the north country dressed like that.

Indeed, when the stranger spoke, his accent had a northern lilt. "Greetings to you! Madoc the Wayfarer, at your service."

Sir Palamon looked the stranger up and down. "And what sort of service might that be?"

"News," said Madoc. "And wonders for my supper."

Randal saw Sir Palamon begin to smile. "A magician, eh?"

"A wizard," corrected Madoc.

Randal stared. For all that the northerner went unarmed and on foot, he'd spoken back to Sir Pala-

mon as if he were an equal. Even Walter, who was the lord's son and almost a knight, couldn't get away with talking to the master-at-arms like that.

Sir Palamon only nodded, though. "Then you're doubly welcome, Master Madoc."

The two men walked together past the stables and the smithy to the castle tower, leaving Randal staring. *So that's a real wizard,* he thought. He'd never seen a wizard before—unless he counted the heal-wife down in the village—and Madoc's arrival filled him with a strange kind of prickly excitement, like life returning to an arm or leg that had gone to sleep.

That night, in the smoky great hall of Castle Doun, it was Randal's turn to wait on the high table, where Lord Alyen had given the wizard an honored place beside Sir Iohan, the oldest of the castle knights. All through dinner everyone talked about politics and looked grim. Randal supposed there might have been a time when the state of the king-dom didn't make people frown and shake their heads, but he couldn't remember things being any other way. King Robert's only daughter had van-ished mysteriously from her cradle the year before Randal was born, the king himself had died the year after, and the dukes and earls had been quarreling over the crown ever since.

As soon as Randal had cleared away the empty plates, Lord Alyen turned to the wizard and said, "Our table talk's been gloomy tonight, Master

Madoc. If your spells can lighten the air somewhat, the rest of us will be grateful."

Randal felt his skin tingle with excitement. This was what he'd been hoping for ever since Madoc had spoken back to Sir Palamon and named himself a wizard—magic. True magic.

The wizard stood up and bowed to Lord Alyen and to the ladies present. Then he came out from behind the high table to the middle of the hall and spoke a sharp word of command. All the torches in the hall went out.

For a moment darkness reigned. Then, out of nowhere, colored lights appeared. Music sounded, softly at first and growing louder, unearthly melodies played on instruments Randal had never heard before. Colored globes and streamers materialized and danced about in time to the music, weaving patterns of light up and down the length of the great hall. The music ended on a final haunting chord, the lights faded away, and Madoc spoke another word. The torches flamed into life again.

The men and women in the great hall burst into applause, but Randal stood motionless, still caught up in the wizard's creation. A great sense of awe and wonder swept over him, making him almost lightheaded for a moment. *How does it feel,* he wondered, *to call something like that out of the thin air?*

At the high table Lord Alyen nodded his approval and said, "You've given us beauty, Master Madoc, and I'd be the first to call that more than enough— but these are troubled times. Can you give us a glimpse of the future as well?"

6

"Usually," said Madoc, "the future is something better left unseen, and most prophecies are too obscure to be useful. But for you and your household, Lord Alyen, I'll do my best." The wizard looked around the hall. "Could someone fetch me a bowl? Wide and shallow, if you have one."

Before any of the other squires could move, Randal had already ducked into the alcove off the side of the great hall. He went straight for the wooden cupboard that held all the serving dishes, and pulled out a large platter of dark earthenware. He carried the platter back into the hall.

"Will this do, Master Madoc?"

The wizard gave the platter a quick glance. "Excellent," he said. "Hold it for me, would you? There's a good lad."

Madoc opened the leather pouch at his belt and took out something small—a piece of crystal, Randal thought. Keeping the small object clenched in his right hand, the wizard moved his closed fist over the empty dish and began to chant in a language Randal had never heard.

The platter turned cold in Randal's hands, and a mist formed above the dark surface. Beyond the wizard, the candles on the high table flickered and burned blue. Randal felt a cold wind ruffle his hair. The gray mist thickened and swirled, and the dish grew suddenly heavier—water filled it up to the brim.

The candles on the table burned high again. Their reflections danced on the surface of the water.

7

Under the lights, the water was dark . . . *No, wait. I see some color,* Randal thought.

Green—it was deep green, rich as a field after a summer rain, bright as a jewel. The patch of green spread until it covered the bottom of the bowl. Randal saw that the color was the bright green of close-cropped turf, and across the turf hooves were pounding, the hooves of black horses. Time passed while Madoc's deep voice rose and fell in meaningless words, and the black horses continued to gallop without sound against the field of green.

The wizard uttered one final harsh syllable. The picture vanished, leaving Randal staring into the empty dish. He shook his head and looked up. Madoc was standing beside him, and the others in the great hall were gazing at the kilted northerner with expressions ranging from amusement to barely concealed awe.

Randal's hands shook. This hadn't been like watching the display of colored lights; this time, the magic had called to something within him, and something had answered.

At a nod from Lord Alyen, Randal returned the platter to the cupboard and resumed his usual place next to Walter. As the noise in the hall grew louder, Randal nudged his cousin and whispered, "Did you see it?"

He waited, still shaking a little, for the answer— he didn't know what had happened, but he knew he had to find out if his cousin had seen the same vision. *What if he hadn't,* Randal wondered. *What if no-*

8

*body else saw it but Madoc . . . or what if nobody saw it
but me?*

But Walter only gave him an odd look. "See what?
Were you daydreaming again?"

He didn't see anything, thought Randal. *And I did.*
The knowledge made him uneasy; he didn't know
what it meant, but he knew it was important. Aloud,
he said only, "I guess I wasn't paying attention.
What happened?"

"What else is new?" asked Walter. "All right . . .
the wizard gave a little speech about everybody
here. You should have seen Sir Palamon grin when
the wizard told him he was going to be in a battle
that would gain him fame enough to last to the end
of his days."

Randal wasn't so sure that was a good fortune—
not without a prediction of just how many those
days were going to be—but he knew from experience that Walter wouldn't see it that way. "Did he
say anything about me?" Randal asked.

"No, he didn't say anything about you," answered
his cousin. "Most of the stuff he did say was good,
though—Father was pleased."

After dinner, Randal sat down and waited at the
foot of the winding stair that led to the upper floors
of the tower. Lord Alyen had given his unexpected
guest a room upstairs, not just sleeping space on the
hall floor; Randal planned to catch the wizard on his
way up to bed. Before too long, the wizard came out
of the great hall and paused at the foot of the stairs.

"Good evening, lad," said Madoc. "What's on
your mind?"

9

Randal stood up. "When you looked into the water tonight, Master Madoc, what did you see?"

"What did I see? The future, of course."

Randal felt his ears beginning to burn with embarrassment, but he'd already said too much to stop now. "Yes—but what did it look like? All I saw was green fields and black horses."

"Not surprising," said Madoc, "with your upbringing."

"But nobody else saw anything at all!" Randal's voice squeaked on the last syllable, and he blushed even redder.

Madoc sighed. "Tell me about the horses, then."

"It was just black horses running," said Randal. He closed his eyes for a moment and tried to remember the picture. A little to his surprise, it came back to him as bright and sharp-edged as before. He watched the scene for a while, and then opened his eyes again. "On a field someplace. Does that mean anything, Master Madoc?"

"Maybe," said the wizard. "Why are you so curious about those horses of yours?"

"Because I saw them," Randal said. "Because nobody else but you saw anything." He paused, took a deep breath, and then went on, feeling foolish and excited at the same time. "Because maybe it means that I can be a wizard, too."

He stopped and stood looking down toward the floor. A moment passed, and then he heard the wizard's gentle laugh. "If I'd juggled three balls after dinner, lad, would you have wanted to be a juggler? Not everyone who sees visions in clear water is

10

meant to work magic. Now run along to bed." With a sigh, Randal did as he'd been told.

Morning came, gray and chilly. Rain fell in sheets across the courtyard of Castle Doun—there would be no sword practice today. Inside the castle, the great hall was busy and crowded, but Madoc didn't seem to want the warmth and company. Randal searched every part of the big, noisy room without luck.

Just before noon, he found the wizard at a turn of the tower stair. Madoc sat in the niche formed by one of the high, narrow windows, reading a small leather-bound book by the light of the gray day outside. No rain blew in—the outer walls of the castle were more than a yard thick—but the cold wind made Randal's teeth chatter. He wondered how the wizard endured it.

Randal asked, "How much longer will you be here?"

The wizard shrugged without turning around. "Until I get tired of staying or Lord Alyen gets tired of having me, whichever comes first." He paused. "One more day, I think."

Only one more day, thought Randal. He got a sinking feeling when he thought of the wizard leaving. Madoc had gone back to his reading; Randal watched him for a while, and then asked, "Do wizards have to read a lot?"

"I never met one who didn't," said Madoc.

"Oh," said Randal. Nobody at Castle Doun could

read, except, perhaps, Lord Alyen. "I suppose I could learn."

"Still wanting to be a wizard, are you?"

Randal nodded. "Yes, sir. Will you teach me?"

The wizard closed his book with a sigh. "Stay here at Doun," he advised. "You've got a bright future ahead of you."

"You never read my future at all," Randal said. "Walter told me so."

"Some things," said the wizard, "are clear enough without needing to look in a puddle of water for the answers. Sir Palamon thinks you'll do well."

"Maybe I don't want Sir Palamon's future," Randal said. "Maybe I want one like yours."

"How can you want to be a wizard, boy? You haven't got the foggiest idea of what it's all about." The wizard rose and stood, glaring down at Randal. The northerner wasn't as tall as Lord Alyen or Sir Iohan, but this close to him, Randal still had to look up to meet his eyes. "You'll spend most of your life with just enough power to get you into trouble. You'll be hungry more often than you're fed, and spend more time in danger on the road than safe under a roof. And maybe you'll survive it all and live to be old and white-bearded and wise—but if you do, most of your friends will have died a long time before. Go back downstairs to your uncle, lad. This is no life for you."

"But—" Randal protested.

"Go downstairs, I said!"

Randal went. The rainy day dragged on, and Randal didn't see the wizard again until dinner.

When the meal was over, Madoc gave the hall a new display of lights and sounds. They were even more beautiful than before, but this time the music was sad. Then a glowing point appeared in front of the wizard, and another and another, shifting and sparkling until they seemed to make a golden tree, with its top three times the height of a tall man.

The tree of light stood for a moment at the height of its glory, its branches full of blossoms. Then, as Randal watched in dismay, it shrank to a gnarled old age, shed its glittering leaves, and decayed into darkness.

Instead of seeking out company after supper, Randal headed for the small room that he shared with Walter. He flung himself down on the bed without bothering to undress, and lay staring up into the dark. Madoc's illusion had made him feel restless and uneasy—he couldn't help feeling that there was a message in it for him somehow.

But what kind of message? he wondered. *Does it mean that if I study magic my life will come to nothing? Or does it mean just the opposite?*

Randal turned the question over and over in his mind, but found no answer. He was still thinking when he fell asleep.

By next morning, the rain had stopped. Randal could smell the clear day coming almost before he awoke: a mixture of clean-washed stone, new grass, and damp earth drying in the sun. He rolled out of bed and stood for a moment, blinking at an empty room.

I'm late again, he thought. *Walter's already gone.*

13

He hurried out the door and down the stairs. Nobody in the great hall stopped him or even seemed to notice him. He walked out into the courtyard. The ground inside the walls lay empty under the bright morning sun, and the castle stood open. Without really knowing why, Randal went through the gate and down to the meadows below.

He didn't go far; only to a low, grassy hill in a field close by the castle. He climbed to the top of the little hill, and lay there looking up at the clear blue sky.

A rumble of sound caught his attention. Faint, but distinct, he could hear it: the noise of many hooves galloping. He sat up and turned to look in the direction of the sound. Far in the distance, a group of horsemen were riding toward him, their banners making bright patches of color against the emerald green of the land.

Randal felt panic rising up to choke him. *The riders are coming for me,* he thought. *I know they're coming for me.* If he stayed on top of the hill, they'd spot him . . . if they hadn't seen him already.

He started down the side of the hill. A second later he stumbled backward, his head ringing. He couldn't see the wall that he'd slammed into, but he could feel it, rough stone beneath his fingers. There was no top to it, or none that he could reach even by jumping. There was no gap in it, either; he followed it by touch all the way around the top of the hill.

Panicked, he sank to his knees, his hands pressing outward against the invisible barrier. *They mustn't find me,* he thought. *I have to find a way out. No way*

14

through the wall, no way over—I'll have to crawl under it.

He began tearing up clumps of grass from the springy turf, scooping at the soft earth, digging away as fast as he could at the dirt under the unseen wall. One finger caught on a buried rock; his nail tore and started to bleed. Outside the wall, the hoofbeats sounded like thunder. Randal pulled the jagged rock free of the dark loam and kept on digging. . . .

Then, with a gasp, he woke a second time, and lay shivering in the gray light that comes just before dawn. On the other side of the room, Walter lay snoring.

It was a dream, he realized. But what kind of dream? What did it mean? He got up and hurried to the castle gate.

"Has anything happened since last night?" Randal called out to the guard on duty.

"Nothing much," answered the guard. "Nobody's come through except the wizard."

"The wizard? You mean Master Madoc?"

The guard nodded. "Said he wanted to be gone before he wore out his welcome."

Gone. Randal clenched his fists. The movement hurt; he looked down at his hands, and saw that they were covered with dirt. A trickle of blood ran out from underneath the fingernail he'd split on a rock that only existed in his dreams.

You wanted an answer, he told himself. *Now you've got one. Leave now, or stay forever. Your choice.*

II.

The Road to Tarnsberg

BY LATE AFTERNOON, Randal had left Doun's gray stone battlements far behind. The low sunlight turned the earthen surface of the King's Road a warm golden color as he paused for a moment and looked at the long track ahead of him.

He'd left the castle before full light after dressing for his journey in sturdy boots and a plain tunic, with his warmest cloak folded up and tucked into his belt behind him. How long a journey this might be, he had no idea. The guard at the castle gate had told him which way Madoc had gone, but the wizard might not have stayed on the King's Road for very long.

At Randal's left side, supported by his belt and by a leather strap over his right shoulder, hung a short sword—the only weapon in Castle Doun's armory that he could honestly call his own. His father had given it to him on the day he'd left his family to train for knighthood in the household of his uncle.

By now, Randal supposed, the whole castle knew

16

that he was gone. All day long he'd half expected to hear the sound of hoofbeats on the road behind him, and had been prepared to turn and face Sir Iohan or Sir Palamon or even Lord Alyen himself, riding after him in angry pursuit. But nothing had happened, leaving Randal to wonder if his presence at Doun had been so little regarded that nobody had noticed his departure.

He brooded over the possibility, but kept on walking. The air grew cooler as he trudged along. Near dark, the combined smells of wood smoke and roasting meat came to him on the evening breeze. The odor of food made his mouth water, but in spite of his appetite he didn't go directly up to the campfire. These days, even the King's Road harbored robbers and bandits of the worst sort.

Instead, Randal turned into the woods to the left of the road. He moved silently, as if he were hunting rabbits with his cousin Walter in the hills around Castle Doun, and found the camp soon enough: nothing more than a small fire in a little clearing, tended by a man in the saffron tunic and plain gray kilt of a northern tribesman.

Madoc, thought Randal with satisfaction. He started to step forward and call out the wizard's name, but then he hesitated. Right now, if he wanted, he could still return to his uncle's castle and the only life he had ever known. Lord Alyen would punish him, of course, and not lightly, but whatever tale Randal spun of time spent lost and wandering would never be questioned, and his offense would soon be forgotten.

But if he went on forward, and Madoc didn't turn him away—then for good or ill, his life would be changed forever. For a moment longer he stood undecided, and then he made his choice.

"Hello the camp!" he called, and stepped from concealment amid the undergrowth.

Madoc turned, seeming unsurprised at the sudden shout. Randal walked forward toward the campfire until he stood about twenty feet away from the wizard. Then he stopped, aware of a great and unexplainable reluctance to go any farther.

Madoc made a hospitable gesture with one hand. "Won't you join me for dinner?"

Randal felt a sudden lightness in both body and spirit as the invisible barrier fell away. He took a few steps forward into the ring of firelight. As he did so, he noticed he had crossed a dark line cut into the turf. Madoc repeated his earlier gesture, and the line shone for a second with a faint blue-white glow; Randal saw that it made a circle all around the little clearing. Then the light faded.

Magic, Randal thought, once again feeling the tingle of excitement he had felt in the great hall at Doun. *It's an invisible wall of magic . . . like the one in my dream last night.*

The northerner was the first to speak. "What brings you out this far from your uncle's castle?"

"I want to be a wizard," said Randal.

Madoc shook his head. "I tell you, lad—I'm not the one who can teach you."

Randal knew that Madoc spoke the truth. He remembered a scrap of lore he'd heard from the healwife in Doun village, something about lies and magic not working in the same mouth, and tried again.

"If you can't teach me wizardry, Master Madoc—will you take me where I can learn?"

Madoc smiled, and Randal knew that this time he had asked the right question. "That much I can do," the northerner said. "Before the snow falls, you'll see the city of Tarnsberg and the school for wizards there."

"But it's barely springtime now," protested Randal. "What will I—will we do until then?"

I can't go back to Doun, he thought. *I'll never be able to leave it all twice.*

"We'll be traveling," said Madoc. "We'll follow the King's Road for a while. And *you,*" he added, "will learn enough about reading and writing to get by at the Schola. That, at least, is something I can teach you on the way. Don't worry, lad, you'll be busy enough on this journey."

The northerner proved as good as his word—and Randal found him to be as hard a taskmaster with sounds and letters as Sir Palamon had ever been with sword and shield. Night after night, as the two of them made their way across Brecelande, Randal went to sleep with rows of meaningless scribbles dancing through his brain. Slowly, though, the scribbles took on meaning, and he began to learn.

One evening some three weeks after they had left Doun, Randal and Madoc took shelter from the weather in a burned-out cottage. The day's traveling had not been pleasant. All afternoon they had hiked over a stretch of ground where somebody's army had passed not long before. The peasants who should have been planting the spring crops had all fled or been killed, and horses had trampled over the plowed fields. In the ruins of what had been a prosperous village, the bodies of men and animals still lay unburied.

They pressed on, but by nightfall they had still not left the destruction behind. The deserted cottage where they finally made their camp lacked half its roof and most of the walls on two sides.

Randal was in a fretful mood. All during supper, which had consisted of flat cakes made of oats and water cooked on a hot rock before the campfire, he kept thinking about the burned-over countryside through which they had passed. The barony of Doun had been at peace with its neighbors, but the possibility of war had been Lord Alyen's chief concern for as long as Randal could remember.

The memory of his uncle stirred another of Randal's worries. He sat brooding for a while, with his arms wrapped around his knees, and then said, "I hope nothing's gone wrong back at Doun. If they're looking for me at all, we should have heard some word of it by now."

Madoc looked at the little fire. "You might as well know, lad—the night before I left, I went to your uncle and told him of your future. They know where you'll be."

Randal lifted his head. "You never read my future."

20

"I didn't say that. I said some things were clear enough without it. And your future is one of those things."

"Will you tell me?"

"No. Knowing the future isn't a good thing sometimes, and this is one of those times."

Madoc gathered up sticks, laid them in the cottage's ruined fireplace, and spoke a word. The sticks started to blaze, radiating warmth against the growing chill of the night. Then the master wizard called up a ball of light, illuminating the interior of the cottage. "Now, to your lessons."

But tonight Randal was too distracted to study. After some unpromising starts, Madoc looked up from the page of the book he had been showing to Randal—the same small volume he had been reading in the tower back at Doun. "What you saw today is bothering you, isn't it?"

"No," said Randal. And then, "Yes." And then, as his mind leapfrogged restlessly from subject to subject, he said, "That last night at Doun, I had a dream." Haltingly, he recounted the events as he had dreamed them, and finished, "I've never had another dream as real as that. . . . Does it mean something?"

"Everything means something," answered Madoc. "The trick lies in knowing what that meaning may be. Besides—many things mean more than one thing at once, especially in dreams."

"So what about my dream?"

"The horsemen," said Madoc, "are obvious. If they catch you, you will be locked into the life of a

21

knight and baron. The invisible barrier is magic, which puts far more limits on you than becoming a knight ever would. The magic held you for a time, forcing you to make a decision."

"That's it?" Randal felt disappointed; he'd half expected something more obscure.

"Some of it," said Madoc. "Not all dreams reveal their whole meaning at first sight."

Randal thought for a moment, then asked, "Do you have dreams that are real?"

"Why do you think I became a wizard to start with?" asked Madoc. "I had a dream . . . very real . . ."

The wizard fell silent and looked into the fire. "I saw myself in a house much like this one, sitting beside a fire, much like this, and talking with a young man."

Randal was silent, hoping that Madoc would continue. After a pause, while rain began to fall, he did.

"I had thought that that dream came true years ago, oh, more years than I care to think. I found shelter in an abandoned hut up on the northern border. I was a journeyman then, and four years at the Schola had given me nothing but a confidence in my own powers that I didn't deserve. And as the rain came down, I found that I wasn't the only one who took shelter there. A young knight came in, walked up to my fire, and asked if he could join me. That rain lasted a week, and we got to know each other well. He said he was Robert, the Warden of the Northern Marches, that his father was the High King, and he would be High King one day."

The wizard stirred the fire, his eyes far away.

" 'So you're the son of the High King,' I said, 'and I'm the King of Elfland's second cousin.' I don't think either one of us believed the other. If he was the Warden, then his job was to protect the borders of Brecelande from my people, and he would never have befriended a tribesman. But it turned out that he had spoken nothing but the truth."

Again the wizard paused.

"While he was High King, there was no war inside the realm. No burned villages, no bands of outlaws. But he died fourteen years ago. And there's been no peace since.

"Why did I want to be a wizard? Not to see the things I've seen, I'll tell you that."

Madoc stood, walked to the broken wall, and gazed into the dark night. The rain continued, harder than before.

At last Randal dared speak again.

"That tree of light you showed us back at Doun," he said. "Did that have a meaning, too?"

"Yes," Madoc replied in a tired voice. "I was asking you if you wanted to let the fruits of your mind wither within stone walls. Now sleep."

Randal rolled up in his cloak and lay by the fire. For as long as he could stay awake, he watched the wizard, but Madoc did not move or speak again that night.

Autumn deepened, and still the journey went on. Randal and Madoc passed from high moorland through wilderness, and across a range of steep hills. They began to pass fields bare from harvesting, and frost lay on the grass in the cold mornings. At last, the road went over a crest that overlooked a gray stone city on a half-moon bay.

Randal stood in a saddle between two hills and gazed down at more buildings than he had ever seen clustered in one place before. *Doun village is nothing by comparison,* he thought. *It could fit into the market square of someplace like this.*

At his shoulder, Madoc said quietly, "Here, if anywhere, you can learn the beginnings of magic: Tarnsberg, home of the Schola Sorceriae."

"The what?" asked Randal. He recognized the phrase as coming from that unknown language in which Madoc sometimes worked his spells, but the words still made no sense.

"The Schola Sorceriae," repeated Madoc. "In the Old Tongue, it means the School of Wizardry."

"The Old Tongue," said Randal. He'd never heard the term before. "Is that magic?"

Madoc shook his head. "No, lad. Merely a language spoken long ago in the countries to the south. All wizards use it—it gives them a common speech wherever they may come from."

"Will I learn it, then?" asked Randal.

"You learned to read, didn't you?" the northerner inquired, and Randal had to nod.

"Well, then," said Madoc, as if Randal's agreement had settled the issue. "It's time to see if the Schola will take you. Come along, lad."

He started down the long hill, and Randal followed, frowning a little at the wizard's kilt-covered back.

24

If the Schola will take me, he thought. So far, he hadn't considered that his long journey might prove useless. The prospect chilled him. *Where will I go if the wizards won't have me?* he wondered. *What will I do?*

Once inside the city walls, he had no time to wonder. Tarnsberg was noisy and crowded—and smelly—in contrast to the clean solitude of Brecelande's open countryside, and Randal stuck close to Madoc as the northerner made his way through the narrow, twisting streets. At last they came to a tavern, a tidy and prosperous-looking place under the sign of the Grinning Gryphon. Its front door stood open to receive the day's customers. Madoc entered and Randal followed.

After the street, the common room of the Grinning Gryphon seemed dim and cavelike. The air inside smelled of ale and smoke and roasting meat. Already, Madoc was talking with an aproned man who stood by the kitchen door. Randal, who had not eaten since breakfast, began to think hopeful thoughts.

While he waited he looked about. Like everything else in Tarnsberg so far, the Grinning Gryphon could have held two or three taverns from the smaller country towns. Light filtered in from the windows opening on the street, and Randal saw that the tavern didn't lack for customers.

In one corner a group of young men and women sat around a single table, all of them listening intently to the older man who paced back and forth near the table's head, talking all the while. The man

25

wore a floor-length tunic of sky-blue satin—its gold trim and flowing sleeves almost as outlandish as Madoc's northern garb—but most of his audience wore plain, and often threadbare, clothing. All of the young people wore loose black robes over their regular garments; Randal wondered if the robes had some sort of significance.

Years of serving dinner at Lord Alyen's table had taught him the knack of listening to a conversation without appearing to eavesdrop. He exercised that skill now, and realized with surprise that he was listening to a class. The man in blue was lecturing in a deep, heavily accented voice on the practice of magic.

"What, you will ask, is the life-force? That is what drives magic, what makes it possible." The man in blue paused, while the young people scribbled furiously on scraps of paper and in small leather-bound books. "Everyone and everything," he went on, "contains that life-force. Ours is more highly developed, simply because we are aware of it. Now"—the man in blue pointed at one of the listeners—"what is the best symbol of the life-force?"

"Blood, Master," said the girl. "Because once all the blood is gone, the life is gone as well."

The man in blue nodded. "Yet there are magical artifacts in the world which have a life-force," he said, "but which are not living things. The blood is in fact a symbol, nothing more—but it is a potent one. How many of you have at least heard of other planes of existence? The farther you go from your own plane of existence, the more difficult it is to re-

26

main where you have gone, and the more difficult it is to have power. For this reason, the planes of chaos and order have little influence on us here. But if a denizen of one of those existences gets a taste of blood . . . and the life-force of which the blood is a symbol . . . its power in this world can be immense."

Randal couldn't quite make sense of everything the man was saying, but he was fascinated nevertheless. He would have listened further, but at that point Madoc arrived with food: two meat pies, still piping hot and oozing gravy, and a pitcher of dark brown cider. The boy and the wizard found seats at an empty table, and Randal dug in. He'd just drained the last of the cider from his mug when the man in blue satin slid into an empty seat at the same table.

"Madoc, you old sheep thief, what brings you here?"

Randal almost choked on the cider he'd been swallowing. Even Lord Alyen had spoken to Madoc with more respect than had this gaudily dressed stranger. But Madoc only laughed.

"Something I found on my travels, Crannach," the northerner answered, and then switched to a language Randal didn't understand, except to recognize that it was neither the Old Tongue nor the language of Brecelande.

While the two men carried on a long conversation, Randal used the opportunity to look around the room. The group of young people who'd been listening to the man in blue had broken up; now

27

they sat alone with books and papers, or talked seriously in small groups of two or three. They didn't have the easy air of Madoc and his new companion—in fact, they all looked tense and worried.

Student magicians? Randal wondered. *Why are they all so grim?* Their somber faces gave him pause; if he became a student himself, he might find out why so few of them were smiling.

Madoc's voice brought Randal out of his reverie. "Well, lad, I'd like you to meet my friend Master Crannach. He agrees that we should introduce you to the Regents of the Schola."

Randal looked from Madoc to the man in blue. "You mean there really is a chance that I can learn magic?"

"Oh, yes," said Master Crannach. "If the Regents will have you, and you can find a teacher who will take you, and you have the strength within yourself to do it."

He gave Randal a penetrating look. "Master Madoc tells me that you lack preparation, and that you have only recently decided to study the art. That won't make your time with us any easier, I fear. But if you're truly suited to the life, then the Schola is the only place for you."

III.

Schola Sorceriae

FOR THREE DAYS, Randal stayed at the Grinning Gryphon, sleeping in one of the small upstairs rooms and spending the rest of his time in the common room listening while Crannach talked to his groups of students. Madoc came and went on business of his own, without explanation.

On the morning of the fourth day, the wizard roused Randal at dawn and stood by while the boy dressed. Outside, the sky was just beginning to go gray above the streets, and the last of the morning stars still burned. Randal and Madoc walked in silence to a tall stone building near the middle of town. They went up a short flight of broad, shallow steps to a heavy wooden door. It was closed, and carved figures of men and women looked down at Randal from their niches between the narrow, glass-paned windows to either side.

At the top of the steps, Madoc paused and turned toward Randal. "This morning you will go before a group of wizards—the Regents of the Schola.

They will ask you questions. Be respectful and tell the truth."

"What will they ask?"

Madoc silenced Randal with a gesture as the door swung open. A hooded figure stood just inside, beckoning to Randal. Madoc gave Randal a slight push.

"This is where I have to leave you, lad—good luck."

Randal stepped across the threshold, and the great door closed behind him. He followed his unspeaking guide up a long stairway. Grotesque carvings of manlike beings and unnatural animals—so detailed that they could have been taken from life—supported the wooden handrail. On the upper floor, the guide halted outside another closed door. They stood there in silence for a long time.

Then, without sound or warning, the door swung wide. Randal saw a large room, longer than the great hall at Doun and almost as high. Shelves full of books filled the whole chamber from floor to ceiling. The milky light of early morning filtered down through high, glazed windows, but most of the room's illumination came from a pair of many-branched candlesticks standing on a table near the far end of the room.

Five people sat in carved, high-backed wooden chairs on the other side of the table. Two were old—at least, the man and the woman who sat in the center of the row had silver hair and lined faces. The third Randal already knew: Master Crannach, whom he had met at the tavern. The fourth man seemed much younger, no older than some of Lord Alyen's household knights, with thick golden hair and a handsome, unmarked face.

The fifth man was Madoc. The other four wizards wore heavy, velvet-trimmed robes of rich black cloth, with deep hoods thrown back to reveal linings of vivid satin. The northerner still wore his familiar gray kilt and saffron tunic, but a similar robe hung over the tall chair back behind him, and Randal didn't doubt that it was Madoc's by right. His friend and guide must be a powerful wizard indeed, he realized, if he sat as an equal with the Regents of the Schola.

The silent, hooded messenger led the way to a spot in front of the table. Then the messenger faded back into the shadows, leaving Randal to stand there alone.

For a long time, there was silence. Randal stood without fidgeting, as he had been trained to do in his days as a squire, and waited. At last, the oldest man spoke.

"I see you wear a sword," he said.

Randal nodded and stood silent.

After another long pause the wizard said, "Throw it away."

Slowly, Randal unbuckled his swordbelt. The short sword had been given to him before his fostering at Castle Doun; it had belonged to his father before him, and to his father's father. Now Randal held it in its sheath—feeling the weight of it, knowing in the core of his being exactly how it felt in his hand, how it swung, where it balanced. Then he tossed it

31

aside and heard it clatter on the stone floor as it landed.

The metallic echoes died away, leaving Randal feeling alone and naked. Into the silence Madoc spoke, his voice suddenly that of a stranger and not Randal's traveling companion of the past months.

"Why do you want to be a wizard?"

Randal looked at the northerner. That was a question that Madoc had asked him before, a question to which he still had not learned the answer. In desperation, he gave the only reply that had so far occurred to him.

"Because I don't want to be anything else."

The blond man at the other end of the table gave Madoc a look Randal could not interpret, and then asked, "How many books have you read?"

"None, Master."

"Then your studies will bear hard on you," said the blond man, with seeming regret. "Most students, before they come here, have read at least one volume."

Master Crannach beckoned to Randal. "Come here, boy."

Randal stepped up to the table. Somewhat to his surprise, Crannach handed him a mirror—a fine one, made of real glass and not just polished metal.

"Hold this," said the wizard. "Don't let it go unless I tell you."

Randal nodded. "Yes, Master."

He stood for a moment and felt the mirror begin to grow warm in his hand. The handle grew warmer and warmer, then hot, then burning. The whole

32

mirror began to glow, its blue-white light streaming between his fingers. Randal bit his lip, seeming to hear the voice of Sir Palamon back in the courtyard at Castle Doun on the day Randal had broken his collarbone during sword practice: *A knight does not cry out in pain.*

Randal shifted his gaze back to the group at the table before him. *And neither does a wizard,* he insisted to himself. *If I drop the mirror now, I'll never be a wizard at all. . . .*

He was so intent on his internal struggle that at first he didn't feel the mirror beginning to change. The handle no longer felt burning hot. It felt cold and thick, and growing thicker. And then it moved.

No longer did Randal hold a simple mirror. A long green snake coiled around his arm. It flicked its tongue, hissed once, and struck.

The fangs sunk deep into Randal's neck. He knew a second of excruciating pain, and then a feeling of numbness started to spread up into his face and down through his chest and arms. Then his hands began to lose sensation as well. Desperately, he hung on to the creature's scaly, writhing body.

If I drop it, I'll never be a wizard. . . .

The spreading numbness reached his eyes. The room blurred around him and went black. Just before all awareness faded, he seemed to hear Madoc's voice speaking words of authority in the Old Tongue.

In the same moment, Randal's vision cleared. The mirror in his hand was once again only a mirror, re-

flecting no more than his own pale and frightened face.

Randal stared, shaken, at his own reflection. As if in a dream, he heard the old man speaking again.

"You have been admitted to the Schola—on probation. Do you know why you were asked to throw your sword aside?"

"Because wizards don't use weapons," Randal replied. "Everybody knows that."

"And it's true enough, as far as it goes," said the wizard. "But the action also symbolized the end of your old life and the beginning of the new. You must put the things of childhood behind you."

Randal barely stopped himself from grinning. He could just see Sir Palamon splutter at the thought of someone calling a sword a "thing of childhood."

The woman in the group spoke for the first time. Her gaze was clear and unwavering, and Randal felt as if she had somehow sensed his thoughts.

"There are some things that must be explained to you," she said. "First, you must never attack or defend with sword or dagger or any knightly weapon. Their use is forbidden to practitioners of the mystic arts. And, second, you must never speak anything other than the truth."

That's easy, Randal thought.

The woman looked sad. "No," she said. "It isn't."

That brought Randal up short. *Can she* really *hear my thoughts?*

"No," said the woman. "I'm not reading your mind. Every student has the same thoughts when he or she is newly arrived here. Consider this to be your first lesson: not everything is a manifestation of power."

With that, the interview seemed to be over. The messenger who had escorted Randal upstairs for the examination reappeared and led him out of the building into a cloister running along the outside of the long hall. Randal could smell cooking odors coming from somewhere ahead, and could hear the sound of voices.

Once the two of them had reached the end of the cloister, the silent guide halted and pushed back his hood. Randal saw a smiling young man, only a year or so older than his cousin Walter back at Doun.

"Hello there," the young man said. His accent sounded strange to Randal's ears—neither Madoc's northern lilt nor Crannach's somewhat harsher tones. "As long as we're going to be here together awhile, we might as well get acquainted. Who are you?"

"I'm called Randal."

The young man looked curious. "That's all?"

Randal thought about it for a minute. He'd chosen to become a wizard without consulting his family, and somehow it didn't seem fair to use their name.

"Just Randal, for now," he said.

The young man nodded, seeming unsurprised. "I'm Pieter, from off south a ways." He smiled and made a little bow. "I was apprenticed to Mistress Pullen before I went off journeying—she's the woman you just met. Now that I've come back to be examined for mastery, she taps me for little jobs sometimes—'Since you're not in classes anymore, and you don't seem to spend your time studying, come do some work for me.' "

Pieter mimicked the voice of the woman who had questioned Randal. The imitation was so accurate that Randal had to laugh. Then, suddenly aware of what he was doing, he stopped.

"Oh, don't worry," Pieter said. "If laughing makes you comfortable here, so be it."

Pieter led the way through the cloister into another building. They went up a steep wooden staircase that climbed almost to the rafters, three floors above the street. The upper area was partitioned into smaller areas by curtains hanging from the roof beams.

Looking out of the dormer windows on this level, Randal could see that the Schola was not, as he had thought, a single structure. Instead, it was a hodge-podge of buildings in different sizes and styles, put together every which way and connected by low walkways, arches, and smaller buildings.

In the middle of the long room, Pieter halted and called out, "Hey, Boarin!"

"What do you want?" answered a cranky voice from behind one of the tapestries.

A hand reached out and pulled back the curtain, revealing an alcove formed by one of the windows. In the alcove, a young man sat tilted back in a heavy wooden chair, a large book lying open on a table in front of him. He scowled at Pieter. "Can't you see I'm busy?"

37

"Not when you're hiding," Pieter answered. "What do you think I am, a magician?"

Boarin gave him a sour look. "A thousand jesters are looking for patrons, and you tell jokes for free. What is it you need this time?"

"A room for my friend here," said Pieter. "This is Randal, and he's just arrived."

"Put him in with Gaimar," Boarin answered. "That's the only room that doesn't have at least three people in it already. Now, if you don't have any serious questions for me, I have to present an illusion tomorrow for Master Laerg."

"Who was that?" Randal asked as the two headed down the stairs. "And who's Master Laerg?"

"Boarin?" said Pieter. "He's already done with his examinations. Right now he's working on his masterpiece—that's the bit of magic you show to the masters to prove that you're worthy to be called a master, too—and the Schola gives him room and board in exchange for supervising the younger apprentices. As for Master Laerg, you've already met him."

Randal thought back to his meeting with the Regents. "Which one was he?"

"The fair one on the end," said Pieter, "sitting as far as he could get from Master Madoc." He shook his head. "Two of the best wizards the Schola's turned out in this century, and they mix like oil and water. Mark my words, we won't be seeing much of your northern friend as long as Laerg's a teacher here."

Randal felt a twinge of apprehension. He'd been

counting on Madoc to see him through the first days of this new and unfamiliar life. And somehow, it didn't seem right that master wizards should feud and disagree like a pair of back-country barons arguing over a misplaced boundary stone.

Randal reminded himself that he didn't know anything about how master wizards behaved among their peers. Pieter, at any rate, didn't seem to find anything surprising in the coolness between Madoc and Master Laerg.

At the bottom of the stairs, Pieter stopped outside a door built into the closed stairwell. "Now that we've got you a room," he said, "let's see about getting you a robe and a book."

He opened the door, revealing a long closet full of shelves. Stacks of folded black garments lay on the upper levels; down below, Randal saw rows of identical leather-bound books, sturdy enough to endure much wear and small enough to fit into a knapsack or a deep pocket. Pieter looked Randal up and down with a measuring eye and pulled a robe off one of the middle stacks.

"This is an apprentice's robe," he said, handing the garment to Randal. "You wear it over your regular clothes—that way everybody in Tarnsberg knows you're with the Schola."

Randal slipped his arms into the wide sleeves and felt the robe settle onto his shoulders. He was dressed now like one of the students he'd watched in the Grinning Gryphon; he wondered how long it would take him to start wearing their worried expression as well.

He turned back to Pieter. The journeyman was holding out one of the books. Randal took it and riffled through the stiff parchment pages. Except for about six lines on the first page, the book was blank.

"It's empty," he said.

"Not for long," Pieter told him. "You'll be filling it up yourself as you learn. For now, write your name inside the front cover—you can write, can't you?—and memorize the spell on the first page."

"What does it do?"

"It calms the mind and focuses the concentration," said Pieter. "Once you get it working, that is. Until then, it tends to have the opposite effect. Now, about meals . . . "

Randal listened distractedly to the rest of Pieter's instructions—how to find the dining hall, when and where to show up for his first class. *Once you get it working,* the journeyman had said. It sounded like there was more to a spell than just having the talent and knowing the proper words.

Pieter finished his speech by telling Randal he was on his own until dinnertime. Randal thought of going back upstairs to the dormitory cubicle he'd be sharing with the as-yet-unmet Gaimar, but then went out into the cloister instead. The covered walkway ran along one side of an enclosed garden with a fountain in the middle; he sat down on the broad stone lip of the fountain and looked again at the spell written on the first page of his book.

To his dismay, the words made no sense, even when he sounded out the syllables one at a time. He recalled what Madoc had said about the Old

Tongue being the language of wizardry, and began to understand what Pieter had meant when he spoke of getting the spell to work. *I don't even know what it says,* he thought. *How am I supposed to make it do anything for me?*

He closed the book, and instead watched a pair of fat orange fish going back and forth in the murky depths of the pool. *What have I gotten myself into?* he wondered. *What if Master Crannach and Master Laerg are right, and the work is too hard?* He was still moodily watching the fish swimming in and out of view when he heard somebody come up beside him.

"New around here, aren't you?" said a cheerful voice. "I can always tell."

Randal looked up with a frown. "Who are you?"

"I'm Nicolas," said the newcomer, a young man with the beginnings of a curly brown beard. "My friends call me Nick."

"Are you a master, or what?"

Nick laughed. "Hardly. I'm just an apprentice like all the rest of you."

Randal felt embarrassed—he should have recognized the black robe, a twin to his own new and still-unfamiliar garment. But the young man didn't look insulted, so Randal went ahead and asked, "Do you live in the dormitory?"

Nick shook his head. "I have my own room in the town—most of the senior apprentices do. Not as crowded, and the food is better."

Randal blinked. "Do the people around here complain about *everything?*"

"Well," said Nick, "it helps pass the time. After

41

you've been here a few months you'll be as bad as the rest of us."

"I suppose so," said Randal. He looked again at Nicolas. The bearded man had to be older than either Pieter or Boarin—and not much younger than Master Laerg, who'd sat with the Regents this morning. "How long have you been here?"

"Coming up on eight years," said Nick.

Randal's heart sank. "It takes that long?"

"No," said Nick, "it just takes *me* that long." The older apprentice tossed a loose pebble into the fountain and went on, "I like it here, so I'm putting off leaving for as long as I can. Meanwhile, I have my own room, upstairs from a carpenter's shop. He lets me stay there in return for helping him out—I watch the place when he's out buying timber, for example, and I tell him if it's going to rain or not."

Randal shot him a questioning look, and Nick hastened to explain, "You can't be an apprentice without learning *something*, and I've got the longest unbroken apprenticeship in the history of the Schola."

"What was the shortest?" Randal asked curiously.

"Two years," said Nick. "That was Master Laerg, of course."

"Of course," echoed Randal, thinking of the fair-haired young wizard. "Everybody says he's good."

"He's brilliant," said Nick. "I'll never be his equal. No one else ever will be, either. But let's not talk about that—hasn't anyone bothered to explain to you how this place works?"

Randal shook his head. "Master Madoc and Pieter told me a little, but not much."

The older apprentice sat down beside Randal on the rim of the fountain. "Then let me tell you how the Schola is set up," he said. "The first couple of years you spend going to classes and learning the basics. After that, you have your second-year examinations. Once you pass those, you're ready to study with one of the senior masters—Pullen, for example, or Laerg. But the hardest part comes when your apprentice days are over. Then you go out on the road as a journeyman, and make your own way by magic until you're ready to take your examinations and present your masterpiece to the Regents."

Nick threw another pebble into the fountain. The plump goldfish took flight into the shadowy depths. "A lot of people quit right there," he said. "The kingdom's too disorderly these days for safe traveling; especially when you can't carry steel and don't really know all that much magic. Some of the ones who don't quit never make it back."

The older apprentice looked a bit grim as he finished speaking; Randal, listening, remembered what Madoc had said back at Castle Doun: *Maybe you'll survive it all and live to be old and white-bearded and wise—but if you do, most of your friends will have died a long time before.*

But the momentary shadow had left Nicolas's face as quickly as it had come. He straightened and smiled again at Randal. "You don't have to worry about that yet awhile," he said. "Just making it through your apprenticeship is going to keep you busy enough."

IV.
Sorcerers' Apprentices

RANDAL SPENT THE rest of the day trying to memorize the focusing spell. He tried to tell himself that he was working real magic at last, but in his heart he knew that nothing would happen if he tried to cast the spell instead of merely reciting the words —the syllables lay on the air like a dead weight, and he felt none of the skin-prickling tension that he'd felt when Madoc worked magic at Castle Doun.

By dusk, he could say the words of the spell without looking at the page before him, but nothing more. He understood now why Crannach's students at the Grinning Gryphon had spent most of their time looking worried, and he was beginning to understand why argument seemed to be the main pleasure of all the apprentice and journeyman wizards he'd met so far—*though I still don't understand,* he thought, *why the masters let them get away with it.*

But a remark that Lord Alyen or Sir Palamon would have called impertinent only served, at the Schola, as the starting point for an hour or more of heated discussion, and argument, as Randal soon discovered, was meat and drink to the masters of the art. As it turned out, Randal's first meal in the refectory—the long dining hall where the students ate together, with a master at the head of each table—also gave him his first demonstration of the wizardly love for controversy.

The meal itself was plain and uninspiring: coarse bread, stewed lentils, and boiled greens. Randal ate his portion without complaint, not thinking it a newcomer's place to criticize the cooking. Another student, however, wasn't as reticent.

"Stew, stew, and more stew," the young man muttered, poking at the lentils with his spoon. "The power of the world and its glory, and we can't even conjure up decent food."

The master at the head of the table—his name, Pieter had said, was Tarn—heard the apprentice's comment or, more likely, the disgusted tone of it. "You wonder that we cannot take dead leaves and worms, and transmute them into rare delicacies, eh? Let us discuss this. Suppose I were to do so?"

The wizard closed his eyes and muttered a brief spell. The bowl of greens in the center of the table turned into a roast fowl on a silver plate.

"Now," he said to the apprentice who had spoken, "why do you suppose we don't do this every day?"

The youth looked as if he wished he'd kept silent. "Because you want to teach us humility?" he ventured after a moment.

Master Tarn sighed. "Would that it were possible. No. Does anyone else care to guess?"

No one spoke.

"Come now, someone must have an idea." Master Tarn pointed at Randal. "Why *not* create feasts by magic?"

Randal could feel the eyes of everyone at the table fixed on him. He hadn't expected to find himself involved in such a discussion before he'd even cast a single spell. At last, he fell back on an answer that had seemed too obvious for serious consideration. "Because the feast isn't really there."

Master Tarn looked surprised. "A glimmering of the concept, I'll be bound. A plate of greens, however it may look, is still a plate of greens." He pointed to the roast bird. "As it happens, what we have here remains vegetative matter. No better or worse than it was before."

Randal's mouth watered. He could see the delicate brown meat on the roast and could smell its rich, golden aroma, but he didn't dare to touch it.

"You could eat it," the wizard said, as if Randal had spoken aloud, "and you would believe that you had eaten it, but your body would not be fooled. That is because what you see before you is an illusion, which works on the mind."

One of the masters at an adjoining table turned and said loudly, "Stuff. Utter stuff and nonsense. Illusions don't work on the mind any more than a mirage does. Illusions affect the air, so that you see what isn't there."

Master Tarn turned away from the apprentices to face the other wizard. "I tell you, illusions are waking dreams."

"Not a bit of it," said the second master. "Creatures without minds nevertheless react to properly cast illusions."

"Show me a creature without a mind," challenged Master Tarn. "Even dogs run in their sleep as they dream."

The original question was forgotten, and the discussion grew esoteric as the two masters argued the point. Other masters from the surrounding tables began calling helpful suggestions back and forth. After a while, the illusion lapsed, and the dish of greens reappeared.

"Does this sort of thing happen often?" Randal asked his outspoken neighbor, who had gone back to eating the bowl of lentils that had started the argument.

The apprentice shook his head. "Not much oftener than once a week. No one knows quite how illusions work, and no one has figured out how to prove the matter either way, so sometimes tempers get high."

Across the table, a thin, sallow boy of about Randal's own age sat laughing quietly. Randal looked at him. The other boy wore an apprentice's robe of fine black cloth, and the garments underneath it looked rich and well-made.

"What's so funny?" asked Randal.

The boy shook his head. "You people take all this so seriously."

You people. Randal didn't like the tone of that. He felt his ears beginning to grow hot.

"What do you mean?" he asked, as calmly as he could.

The other boy gave Randal a condescending smile. "You listen to Tarn and Issen as if which way the spell works really makes any difference."

"But it would, I think." Randal frowned at his bowl of lentils and tried to put into words a new and unfamiliar thought. "If you cast an illusion spell and it works on somebody's mind . . . isn't that the same as telling them a lie?"

The other boy shook his head. "Unbelievable— you haven't even been here a whole day and already you're as bad as the rest of them."

Randal couldn't think of an answer to that. Instead, he finished his bread and lentils in silence while the refectory echoed with the arguments of the masters and senior apprentices.

After dinner, he made his way back to the small room Boarin had assigned to him. When he walked in, he wasn't pleased to find the unpleasant boy from the refectory already there and sitting in the tiny room's single chair. The boy had his booted feet propped up on the windowsill.

"What are you doing here?" Randal asked.

"I could ask you the same thing," the boy said without getting up. "I live here. Gaimar, at your service."

"Well, I live here, too," said Randal. "Boarin put me in with you."

Gaimar looked irritated. "He did, did he? That explains why there's a pile of strange junk cluttering up my room."

"Our room," said Randal. He didn't think that one woolen cloak and the walking stick he'd cut for himself on the road added up to a "pile of junk," but his first day at the Schola probably wasn't a good time to argue about it.

The other boy shrugged. "Whatever. You'd better not be one of those work-all-day-and-study-all-night chaps. But if you are, please don't keep me awake talking about it."

"I won't," said Randal shortly.

He found himself disliking the other boy intensely, even on such brief acquaintance, and his dislike didn't grow any less as the days and weeks went by. Gaimar missed as many classes as he attended and seemed to have only scorn for the masters who taught them, but he learned each new spell with an almost casual ease. Nor did Gaimar have much sympathy for Randal's difficulties with reading and writing. The former squire was still struggling with the language of Brecelande—the need to learn the Old Tongue at the same time sent him to bed, night after night, with bleary eyes and an aching head.

In desperation, Randal finally tried putting the new words into lists and reciting them out loud—whereupon Gaimar, who could read swiftly and silently in both languages, accused him of being a distraction and threw him out of their shared room.

Randal wandered gloomily out of the dormitory, his list of words clutched in one hand. He stood for a moment undecided in the cloister, trying to make up his mind where to go next, and then turned to-

49

ward the library. Halfway up the broad wooden staircase with its grotesque carvings, he met his friend Nicolas coming down.

"I hope you're not planning to go into the library," said the older apprentice. "It's closed just now. The Regents are examining a journeyman for mastery this afternoon, so the rest of us have to go somewhere else."

Randal sighed. "So who's the candidate and how are his chances?"

"It's Boarin," said Nick. "And I'd say he doesn't have to worry, we'll be calling him 'Master Boarin' by this evening. In the meantime, the refectory is going to be full of junior apprentices trying to study, and you won't be able to hear yourself think. Why not work over at my place instead?"

A little later, Randal found himself in an attic room over a carpenter's shop on the outskirts of Tarnsberg. A few garments hung from pegs along the wall, a pewter pitcher and a matching mug stood on a rickety table, and a lute hung over the head of the narrow, lumpy bed. Books, scrolls, and magical instruments filled the rest of the tiny space, overflowing their shelves to pile up on the bed and the only chair.

"Welcome to my humble garret," said Nick. "I remember what the first year at the Schola can be like. So if you ever need a place to get away to for a few hours, come by here. I'll tell old John Carpenter that you're a good fellow, and to let you in if I'm not around."

"Thanks," said Randal. After a moment, he said,

"You've been around the Schola for a while. . . . Do you know Gaimar?"

Nick grimaced. "You've run into him?"

Randal nodded. "I live with him. And I don't think he likes me very much."

"Gaimar doesn't like anybody," said Nick. "He's the youngest son of a lord off in the east somewhere, and his family likes the idea of having a wizard in the ranks. He has the talent and the temperament, so they pay room and board to the Schola and send him money to live on—but what he really wants to be is a baron like his father."

"Funny," said Randal. "That's the sort of thing I left home to avoid."

"I thought so," said Nicolas, "and Gaimar probably knew what you were the instant he saw you. He's not going to love you for it, either."

"So what should I do?"

"Ignore him," Nicolas recommended. "As much as you can, anyway."

Randal sighed. "I suppose I could call it practice in maintaining concentration." He unrolled the square of parchment with his list of words, and started reading aloud. *"Fors, fortis, fortem . . ."*

With Nick's attic room for a refuge, Randal slowly began to learn the complicated vocabulary and grammar of the wizards' language. But as Pieter had implied on that first day, there was more to working magic than simply knowing the words.

Several months after Randal's arrival in Tarnsberg, he sat at a table in one of the rooms on the upper floor of the Schola. With him were gathered

51

his classmates—all the apprentices who had come in during the last year. Master Tarn was giving the class today, a lesson in candle lighting. One candle, already lit, burned in a tall, many-branched candlestick beside the lectern. A basket of new, unlit candles lay in the center of the table, and a plain wooden candleholder had been set before each student's place.

The master wizard stood at the front of the room and surveyed the tables full of students. "Why light a candle?" Tarn asked. Nobody said anything, and he went on. "More important, why use magic to do such a simple task?"

He picked up an unlit candle, and reached out with it to touch the wick of the candle burning beside his lectern. The wick of the first candle caught fire, and Tarn set it into an empty socket in the candlestick. "You there," he said to one of the students as he did so, "you don't need to write this part down. I'll tell you what you need to write down. For now, just watch what I'm doing."

The apprentice looked abashed. Randal closed his own book as quietly as he could—he, too, had been about to write down the master's comments.

Tarn went on. "The reasons for learning how to light a candle are threefold. First, it teaches control. You must aim your effect carefully. Second, it teaches technique. If you don't cast the spell correctly, you will know at once—the candle will not burn. Third, and most obvious, knowing how to light a candle without material aids can sometimes be useful."

The master paused. When he had the full attention of all the apprentices, he continued. "One more thing. Until you have developed satisfactory control and technique, do *not* practice this spell in a wooden building without having a master nearby! Now let us begin."

Randal took a candle from the basket in the middle of the table and set it in the candleholder in front of him. He looked at the stubby cylinder of beeswax for a moment, running through the words of the candle-lighting spell in his head.

After enough practice—or so he had been told—reciting the words and making the gestures became unnecessary for such a minor spell. Randal was a long way from that point, but already one of the more advanced apprentices had her candle lit. To show off, she extinguished the flame by magic, conjuring up a tiny puff of wind, and then lit the candle a second time. Her air of satisfaction didn't last long, however; Master Tarn had taken note of her efforts, and responded by running her through a series of even more difficult spells. He finished by causing the candle flame to burn a pure dark green, leaving her with a frustrated expression as she tried to duplicate the effect.

All the while, Randal stared at the cold wick of his own candle. Nothing happened. He recited the words of conjuration again. Nothing. Randal looked around. Everyone else in the room, even apprentices who had arrived at the Schola long after him, had managed to complete the exercise and sat gazing at brightly burning candles.

Randal heard a footstep at his elbow. He turned and saw Master Tarn looking down at him. "What seems to be the problem here, young Randal?" asked the wizard. "Conjuring a flame is one of the easiest spells there is."

"I just can't seem to get it, Master Tarn," Randal admitted in a low voice.

"Tell me the words you're using."

Randal recited the spell. The master listened intently, and then nodded.

"As I thought," said Tarn. "You left out a word. And your pronunciation is . . . unusual, to say the least. Try it again, and this time enunciate."

Randal tried again. Nothing happened.

"Do you spend much time studying your lessons in the Old Tongue?" Master Tarn asked. Before Randal could answer, he went on. "Tell Master Boarin that you are signing up for additional instruction. You need it badly."

Randal wondered where he was going to get the time. In spite of Madoc's lessons on the road, Boarin already had him signed up for extra work in handwriting, reading, and theory. But he knew better than to protest—sleeping and eating apparently ranked low in importance at the Schola, at least for apprentices. "Yes, Master," he said with resignation.

"Now try again," Master Tarn said.

Randal ran through the spell again: the words, the gestures, the thoughts. He concentrated on the candle. For another long minute, nothing happened.

Then the candle bent in the middle and collapsed. The center had melted.

"At least you got some heat that time," Master Tarn commented. He regarded the drooping candle with a sober expression. "Remember, only one candidate in ten who comes to Tarnsberg is allowed to become an apprentice. And of those, only one in ten goes on to become a journeyman. Something to think about."

The master walked back to the front of the room. "Class is dismissed for the day," he said to the apprentices. "Be here again next week at the same time."

Randal began to bundle up his materials. "No," Tarn said. "You stay. And practice until you get it right."

Randal thought he was about to die of embarrassment. But instead he nodded without looking at any of his classmates, and set to work trying to light the candle.

V.

Hue and Cry

IN THE BAY of Tarnsberg, fishing boats came in from the sea each morning across the sparkling dawn. One day in autumn, Randal stood looking from the high window of the dormitory where he stayed, watching the triangular sails catch the red light of the sun as it rose over the hills behind the city.

The rising sun cast a rosy light on the open page of the leather-bound notebook Randal had been working in the night before, until Gaimar had demanded that he put out the candle and go to sleep. Randal's handwriting had improved over the course of the months—almost a solid year—he had been at the Schola, but his script remained almost illegible, and the book's first pages were an outright disaster.

By now, Randal had filled almost half the book's pages with the thoughts and comments of half a dozen teachers, plus a collection of minor spells and incantations. Still, most of the time, even the simplest charms eluded him, and he felt no closer to understanding wizardry than when he had first arrived.

I'll be here twice as long as Nicolas, without ever learning half of what he has, Randal thought as he pulled on his tunic.

During the past year, the old clothes that he had worn from Doun had grown too short and too tight across the shoulders, so he had given them to the Schola in exchange for others. The new garments—probably somebody else's, also outgrown—had proved to be too large, and threadbare as well, but they were warm and serviceable. Randal fastened his belt and shrugged his apprentice's gown on over his shoulders, trusting the black garment to cover most of the patches in his hand-me-down tunic.

Outside the window, the fishermen down in the harbor were furling their sails and drying their nets. In the streets of the city, the bustle of countrymen come to market was just beginning. Randal stood at the window for a moment, watching the peaceful scene. Not for the first time, he wondered how things stood at Castle Doun and how Lord Alyen had taken his sudden departure.

It's been more than a year, he thought. *And nobody's brought a message or come asking for me. Did the Schola send anyone word that I was here?*

He wondered what the folk at Doun had made of his departure, and what they had told his family. *Do they mention my name sometimes, or have they forgotten all about me?*

Sighing, Randal turned away from the window. He picked up a scrap of parchment that had been lying on the table, weighted down by the small piece of rock crystal he used without much success as a focus in memorizing spells. Last night after dinner, Gaimar had handed him the note with a look of ill-concealed satisfaction; most of Randal's concentration, for the rest of the evening, had gone into concealing how much the message had frightened him.

In the morning, the note read, *I will be free. Trouble yourself to find me then: your studies are not progressing in a satisfactory manner. Boarin.*

At first, Randal had thought about finding Nick to ask his advice. Someone who prided himself on serving out the Schola's longest continuous apprenticeship must surely be familiar with messages like that one.

Or maybe not. Whenever he needed to, Nick could perform magic flawlessly. He had a natural talent. By now, Randal was certain that he himself had no such thing. Every gain came with soul-rending effort, and those gains were too few and too small to grant much comfort. Even Gaimar, who regarded wizardry and the Schola with equal disdain, could do better.

Randal cast a disgusted glance at his roommate, still snoring in the room's other bed, and then strode on out into the dormitory. *If Boarin's awake,* he thought, *I might as well get this over with.*

He found Boarin alone in the refectory, eating an early breakfast—the junior master had probably drawn the task of casting the spells that started the cooking fires and otherwise brought the Schola kitchens to life. Back at Castle Doun, Randal remembered, the cook and the kitchen maids had been at work well before sunup every day.

Boarin looked up as Randal came in. "I've been meaning to talk to you," said the junior master. "Sit down."

Randal sat. This close to the refectory kitchen, he could smell the rich aroma of cracked wheat porridge flavored with dried fruit and honey—breakfast today would be good, for a change. But the message from Boarin had destroyed any appetite he might have had.

"I got your note last night," Randal said.

"At least you don't put things off," said Boarin. "That's good." The junior master pushed aside the remnants of his breakfast and folded his hands together on the tabletop. "Randal, I like you. Almost everybody does. But that isn't enough. You just haven't been making progress."

Randal nodded again. *I suppose this is where they throw me out,* he thought, clenching his fists tightly under the table. With an effort, he kept his voice steady. "Yes, sir. I know."

Boarin looked sympathetic. "And we know that it's not really your fault that your preparation was so poor, but that doesn't help now. You're one of the nonpaying students, and that means you're held to a higher standard. The examinations at the beginning of your second year will be coming up soon, and if you can't pass those you'll have to leave. It's not really fair, when the fee-paying students can attend classes for as long as their money lasts—but that's the way the world works."

"I understand," said Randal. "But what can I do?"

The junior master shook his head. "I don't know. Practice as much as you can—work on control and technique. You have considerable natural talent, Randal, and we don't want to lose you because it turns out to be untrainable."

Feeling confused and depressed, Randal made his way out of the refectory and into the streets of Tarnsberg. *So I have a natural talent,* he thought, and laughed without humor. *What good is that to me if I can't learn how to use it?*

He wasn't sure where he wanted to go next. He didn't have a class until the tenth hour, and returning to the dormitory would mean having to put up with a morning full of Gaimar's irritating presence. For a while he wandered aimlessly through the streets. Finally he started across town toward the woodworkers' district, hoping to find Nicolas at home. *Maybe he'll know what I should do.*

"Stop!"

The cry in the distance brought Randal out of his reverie. He halted and looked around. Tall buildings, some of them as high as three stories, crowded in on either side of him, blocking his view and cutting off any way of escape. Then he relaxed a little. He was alone in the street, and the shout came from too far away to be directed at him.

"Stop!" came the shout again. "Stop, thief!"

Then Randal understood. Somebody had started a hue and cry in the marketplace. Now all the law-abiding citizens within earshot would drop their work and chase the wrongdoer—filling the streets, flowing down the alleys and byways. Capture by the mob could be brutal, and the thief would need quick wits and fast legs to get away.

Even as Randal paused, thinking, he heard the uproar of a crowd of people coming in his direction. The voices sounded ugly—not the sort of situation he wanted to get into on a day like today. *If I run,* he thought, *they'll think I'm the one they're after. Better get out of the way.*

He stepped backward into a convenient niche between two close-set buildings—a narrow space large enough to hold only an apprentice wizard and an empty rain barrel.

The mob sounds grew closer, along with the cries of "Stop! Stop, thief!"

Randal grimaced. He'd lived in the city for almost a year now, long enough to know that even people who didn't know or care that a theft had been committed would be joining the hunt.

Anything for entertainment, he thought in disgust. *Especially with a chance of blood at the end.*

Then, over the noise of the approaching crowd, Randal caught the sound of running footsteps. Before he could move, a small, ragged figure dashed into the narrow alcove. The thief, a loaf of fresh bread clutched under one arm, looked from Randal to the blank wall at the end of the alley.

The apprentice wizard got a quick glimpse of a thin, sharply pointed face and large dark blue eyes. Then the fugitive gasped, "Don't let them get me!"

in a breathless whisper, and dived into the rain barrel.

Randal stepped back out into the street and looked in the direction of the market square. Sure enough, the crowd was already pounding up the street. Even the smallest, Randal noted with scorn, was larger than the one who'd asked for his help.

The leaders of the mob thundered up to where Randal stood watching.

"You—wizardling!" called out a burly fellow whom Randal recognized as Osewold Baker, a man who kept a shop near the Schola. "Did you see a boy just now?"

Randal shook his head. "Sorry, no. I haven't seen any boy coming in this direction."

The baker frowned. "Well, you're not the one we're looking for. He must have taken another way." Osewold turned back to the crowd and yelled, "We must have lost him in Pudding Lane!"

He headed back the way he had come. The mob, still shrieking, "Stop!" and "Thief!" reversed itself and went surging after.

When the last of them had gone, Randal strode back to the barrel. Reaching inside, he grabbed a handful of tunic and hauled out the fugitive hiding there—a featherweight bundle of rags on a body that felt like mostly bone.

Randal put himself between the barrel and the mouth of the blind alley. Still holding on to the fugitive's shoulder, he looked his captive up and down.

"Well, now," he said slowly, "aren't you the lucky

one? If they'd asked, 'Did you see a thief come this way,' I'd have had to say yes."

The fugitive didn't look particularly grateful. "Well, why didn't you?"

"Because I can see you aren't a . . . "

But Randal didn't get a chance to finish. The would-be thief wrenched free and made a dash for the street. Randal reached out an arm and caught the back of the fugitive's torn and dirty tunic.

"Because, like I was saying," Randal finished, holding on tighter this time, "I can see you're not a boy."

The girl—unwashed, underfed, and no older, Randal realized with a brief sense of shock, than he was himself—said only, "You've got sharper eyes than that fool of a baker."

"Fool or not," said Randal, "Osewold had sharp enough eyes to spot you stealing that bread. Not a bright idea, in a town where any journeyman can cast a protection spell."

The girl shrugged. "I was hungry."

"Hungry or not," said Randal, "you can't go walking around in those clothes any longer. If anybody recognizes you, they'll call up the mob again and tear you apart."

"It can't be helped," said the girl. "These are the only things I've got."

Randal stood for a moment, thinking. He hadn't intended to take responsibility for a half-starved and unskilled shoplifter—but neither had he been able to turn her over to the justice of the mob.

63

He sighed. *Everything has its consequences, as Master Tarn would say.*

"Come with me," he said. "I know a place near here where you'll be safe—and can get fed, too."

A short time later they were up in Nicolas's room over the carpenter shop. Nick sat on the rumpled bed, trying to tune his lute, and Randal sat cross-legged on the wooden floor. The girl sat in the only chair, tearing hungrily at the loaf of stolen bread, which she held in one hand. In the other hand she held a wedge of cheese that Nicolas had wheedled out of the carpenter's wife.

As Randal watched, the girl bit an enormous half-moon out of the cheese, chewed briefly, and swallowed. Then she pulled off another mouthful of the bread.

"If you eat too fast," Randal warned, "you'll make yourself sick."

The girl nodded and kept on chewing.

"My name's Randal," he said after a moment. "And that's Nicolas."

The girl took a swig of water from a mug that Nick had filled from the pitcher on the table. She swallowed, and then pointed at herself. "Lys."

Before the conversation could go any further, she took a huge mouthful of bread, another of cheese, and began chewing again. Not until she had finished every crumb did she stop and lean back in the chair with a sigh of satisfaction. "Thanks," she said. "That's the first decent meal I've had in many a long day."

Her voice, now that she was no longer fearful or

64

suspicious, proved clear and sweet, and she spoke the language of Brecelande with an unfamiliar—though not unpleasant—accent.

Randal looked at her with curiosity. "Where do you come from?" he asked. "It's plain you're not from around here."

"I'm from the southern lands," she said. "Occitania, Vendalusia, Meridocque . . ."

"Which one?" asked Nicolas. The brown-bearded apprentice was still working over the strings of his lute as he spoke.

"All of them," said Lys, "or none of them. Take your choice." She cocked her head on one side, listening as Nicolas plucked another pair of strings.

"If I live to be sixty, I'll have spent forty years trying to tune this thing," Nick said.

Lys held out her hand for the instrument. "You're never going to do it that way," she said. "Give it to me."

Nicolas handed over the lute, and the two apprentices sat listening for a few minutes as the girl's thin, dirt-stained hands quickly brought the jangling strings back into order.

When the task was finished, she looked up from the instrument and said, "Don't wizards have charms for things like this?"

"We're just apprentices," said Randal.

Nicolas nodded agreement. "Besides, even the masters at the Schola agree it's no use tuning an instrument by magic."

"Why not?" Lys asked.

"Well," said Nick, "just *getting* the lute in tune is

65

easy . . . for some people, anyway . . . but then you have to *keep* it there. Nothing can change in the wood or the strings or the tuning pegs, or else the notes will start changing again. And stopping change means stopping time."

"But you can't have music without time," protested Lys. "It's impossible."

"Exactly," said Nick. The older apprentice looked thoughtful. "I've heard that only elves and demons—who live on planes outside of time—have mastered the art of making instruments that never change their tune."

"Like elfin swords," said Randal. "They never rust or lose their edge."

"That's in the stories," said Lys with a crooked smile. "Real life is different."

Before either of the two apprentices could answer, she began to pick out a tune on the strings of the lute. Then she sang in a clear alto voice:

"Her skirt was of the grass-green silk,
    Her mantle of scarlet fine;
From every lock of her horse's mane
    Hung fifty silver bells and nine."

Randal had heard the song before in the great hall at Doun. This time, though, the story of the mortal man who went off with the Queen of Elfland to be her consort seemed not magical, but sad. By the time the last notes died away among the rafters of the untidy attic room, Randal was blinking back

tears, and Nicolas was staring at Lys with unconcealed respect.

"By the sun, the moon, and all the stars," said the bearded apprentice, "if you can make music like that, what were you doing stealing bread from Osewold's bakery?"

"I was hungry," she said, as she had before back in the alley. "Out in the countryside I could trade my music for food, but my luck ran out when I got to Tarnsberg."

"You came from the Southlands by yourself?" Randal asked.

Lys shook her head. "I was with my family. . . . We were all players, a whole troupe. We could do whatever an audience wanted—songs, dances, even plays—and people used to pay good money to watch us perform. Copper, silver . . . and gold, once, at a duke's wedding. Then we heard that there hadn't been any troupes playing in Brecelande for almost twenty years, so we decided to come north and try out the audiences here."

She raked her hand across the lute strings in a harsh discord. "Two months this side of the Occitanian border, bandits attacked our camp. I'd gone to buy a dozen eggs from a farm wife down the road; when I came back, everybody was dead."

She paused for a moment, her bright blue eyes gone dark as they looked at a scene long past. Then she seemed to pull herself out of her memories and went on speaking. "The bandits had taken everything, even the costumes. They didn't leave as much as a pennywhistle behind."

68

"I'm sorry," Randal said finally, although he knew the words weren't good enough. "I wish . . . "

"Wishing butters no parsnips," said Nicolas briskly. "I'll tell you what, Demoiselle Lys, I'll loan you that lute for as long as you're in Tarnsberg. You can talk the carpenter's wife out of a bath and some clean clothes without much trouble; she's a kind-hearted soul. Then go tell the landlord of the Grinning Gryphon that Nicolas Wariner sent you over to entertain the afternoon crowd."

Lys was beginning to smile again, her thin face seeming to light up from within. Randal, watching her, still couldn't think of anything to say. He knew that the kingdom of Brecelande had fallen on bad times since the High King's death—sometimes, back at Castle Doun, the talk had seemed to be of nothing else. Just the same, the player-girl's tale made him feel helpless and angry as the political discussions had not.

But what can I do? he thought bitterly. *I'm only an apprentice wizard—and not a very good one, at that.*

After showing a cleaned-up and better-dressed Lys the way to the Grinning Gryphon, Randal headed back to the Schola for his tenth-hour class. The interview with Boarin earlier that morning had left him feeling grim and unhappy, and his encounter with the player-girl had only served to worsen his mood.

He wasn't surprised, therefore, when his tenth-hour class turned out to be a disaster. Even his attempts at conjuring up a simple reading light—the cold-flame most apprentices learned to summon by

69

the end of their first year—came to nothing. When, on his ninth or tenth try, a light finally came, the blue-white glare nearly blinded him, and blistered his fingers besides.

"Control," said Master Tarn with a sigh. "You can't approach a minor spell as though you were summoning demons inside a circle. Go get some salve on that hand, then come back, and we'll go over the theory again."

VI.
Storm Clouds Gathering

THE NEXT FEW weeks brought more of the same, and worse. Spells that Randal had found difficult before, he now found impossible. Others, like the reading light, went awry when they worked at all. The prospect of second-year examinations loomed over Randal's existence like an ugly mountain.

Not even Lys's success at the Grinning Gryphon could lift his spirits. The patrons of the tavern, mostly wizards and apprentices, liked her music so much that the innkeeper gave her room and board in exchange for providing entertainment. But Randal, while he felt pleased that Lys no longer had to choose between theft and starvation, found himself jealous as well. The player-girl, at least, had a talent that answered when she called upon it to serve her needs.

But even Lys, who could make music as well as any minstrelsy he'd ever heard, had needed to steal bread to keep from starving, so what might a failed wizard have to do to keep himself alive?

I could go back to Doun, he thought, and then shook

71

his head. It had been a long time since he'd left the castle; a long time since he'd worn the padded practice armor or lifted even a wooden sword. *I've forgotten all I ever learned about becoming a knight—even if they'd still let me—and so far I don't know anything about being a wizard.*

In fact, Randal concluded bitterly, his training so far had only made him useless to everyone, including himself.

It was in that same dark mood, one afternoon in late summer, that Randal came back to the dormitory room he still shared with Gaimar. As usual, Randal's roommate had appropriated the only chair. He sat with his feet on the table, leaning back, summoning up colored bubbles of light, and then popping them one at a time in a shower of sparks.

Randal watched him for a few minutes with mounting irritation. "Is that all you can think of to do?"

Gaimar called forth a handful of golden bubbles and bounced them in the air above his empty palm. "What's it to you, anyway? You can't even do that much."

Randal gritted his teeth. "I'm learning," he said. "And someday . . . "

"Don't hold your breath waiting," said Gaimar. One of the golden bubbles burst with a quick, echoless bang. A shower of gold flecks sifted down, circling among the bubbles that remained. "You've been here more than a year and you haven't even managed to light a candle."

Randal said nothing. He flung himself down on

72

his cot and stared up at the dimness among the rafters. On the other side of the room, he could hear the sound of three more bubbles popping in quick succession.

"Stop that," he said finally.

Gaimar snickered. A half-dozen gold and silver bubbles sprang into existence over Randal's head. They dodged and flitted about like fireflies, breaking apart in showers of glittering dust whenever their paths collided.

"I said stop that," said Randal.

"Why should I?"

"Because if you don't," said Randal, "you're going to regret it."

A silver bubble floated down to a spot just above Randal's nose, hovered there for a moment, and then burst. Randal came up off the cot and onto his feet in one smooth motion. Gaimar still had his feet propped up on the table. As Randal stood, the other apprentice looked around from calling up another cluster of colored lights.

"Just what do you think you're going to do?" asked Gaimar. The lights all broke at once, in a flash of color.

"This," said Randal, and kicked the chair out from under him.

Gaimar scrambled to his knees, his features contorted with rage. "I'll teach you, you no-talent, mannerless . . . "

He pulled a handful of flame out of the air and threw it at Randal.

Gaimar's magic was better than his aim. The fire-

73

ball missed. Flame singed the hair on Randal's head as the fireball flew past and hit the curtains.

Furious now, Randal flung himself upon the other apprentice, and Gaimar, wizardry forgotten, fought back with fists, feet, and teeth. The two youths rolled about on the floor, pummeling each other and banging into the furniture.

Abruptly, Randal felt himself being grabbed by an invisible hand and yanked away from his opponent. Ungently, the hand let him fall on the floor a few feet away from Gaimar. Randal looked up, breathing hard, and saw Boarin standing in the center of the long dormitory. Behind the junior master, the curtains smoked where the fireball had struck the heavy cloth.

Boarin's face was stern. "What was all this about?" he inquired. "And why are two apprentice wizards brawling with fists like a pair of common stable-boys?"

Randal pulled himself to his feet again. *Take your discipline standing up, boy,* he seemed to hear Sir Palamon's voice echoing in his mind. *A knight doesn't grovel before any man.*

After a few moments, Gaimar stood up also. Boarin looked from one youth to the other. "All right . . . who started it?"

For a moment, there was silence. *A wizard never tells anything but the truth,* thought Randal.

"I started it," he said.

Boarin gave Randal a penetrating glance. "I see. Do you care to explain why?"

Randal thought about Gaimar's carelessly broken

bubbles, about Madoc's creations of light and sound that had first shown a wide-eyed squire the wonders of magic, and about the hard-learned craft of the player-girl Lys. Any explanation he could make would only be a mixed-up jumble of all those things, and no real reason at all . . .

"No, sir," he said.

"I see," said Boarin again. His glance moved to the scorched curtains and back to the two apprentices. "Brawling in the dormitory is a serious offense, and I should report both of you to the Regents. However . . . I think we can avoid that this time, if the two of you can find separate quarters."

Randal nodded. He knew as well as anybody that the dormitory was full. "In town, you mean?"

"If necessary," said the junior master.

Gaimar looked smug. "My father's already paid my board to the Schola for this year."

Boarin gave him a reproachful look. "I had thought—"

"Never mind," said Randal before Gaimar could say anything. "I can find a place in town."

Nick will know of a room somewhere, he told himself. *And if he doesn't, Lys probably will.*

Randal didn't bother going to dinner in the refectory that night. Instead, he made his way to the woodworkers' section of Tarnsberg, where Nicolas kept his upstairs room in the carpenter's shop.

"Why the long face?" asked the bearded apprentice as soon as Randal made his appearance. "What's wrong?"

Randal threw himself down onto the single chair. "I had to leave the dormitory."

"You?" Nick sounded puzzled. "What happened?"

Randal shrugged. "I got in a fight with Gaimar."

"Bound to happen someday," was all Nick said. After a moment or two of silence, he added, "Gaimar's family can afford to rent him rooms anywhere in Tarnsberg. So why are you the one moving out?"

"Because I was the one who started the fight," said Randal. He didn't feel like explaining any further right now, even to a friend like Nick. "So I came here to find out if you knew any empty places around town. . . . Any cheap places," he added, "since I'll have to pay the rent out of odd jobs and errands."

Nick gave his friend an odd look. "If anybody ever doubts that you're going to make a master wizard someday, your timing ought to convince them otherwise."

Something about the tone of Nick's voice made Randal uneasy. "What do you mean?"

"Not much," said Nick. "It's just that this place is going to be empty tomorrow morning."

"What?" asked Randal.

He looked about the attic room. With his mind diverted from his own problems, he could see now that the familiar clutter had a different look to it—as if Nick had been sorting things out for packing or throwing away. All the dozens of books had been stacked in bundles and tied together with cords, and the usually scattered garments lay neatly folded on the bed.

"Don't tell me," Randal said. "You've finally given in and let them make you a journeyman wizard."

"Not exactly," said Nick. "I had a long talk with old John Carpenter last night. He's got a cousin in the carpentry trade up north in Cingestoun, and it seems that the cousin needs a new man to help him out, and maybe someday take over the shop, seeing that there aren't any sons or nephews."

Randal stared at him. "You're going to go apprentice yourself to a carpenter?"

"A bit better than that," said Nick. "Old John's already gone to ask the Guild to make me a journeyman. He says I've picked up more of the trade helping him out part-time than most apprentices do in their whole term."

"But—you're leaving magic?" Randal felt dizzy and confused. "Why?"

"The world can always use a good carpenter," said Nick, "and I've played at wizardry long enough. If I'd ever really wanted the magic, I'd have been on the road years ago."

Randal searched his friend's face. Nick meant what he said; that was clear. "You're leaving tomorrow?"

"That's right," Nick said. "There's a salt merchant's pack train going north in the morning, and I can travel with them if I'm ready in time."

"Well . . . good-bye, then." Randal tried not to sound upset. He hadn't realized before how much he'd depended on Nick's advice to get him through day-to-day life at the Schola.

"Don't look so glum," said Nick. "I'm going over to the Grinning Gryphon to tell Lys she can keep the lute—want to come along?"

"I don't think so," said Randal, thinking that he was in no mood for the cheerful inn. "But I'll wait here for a while, if you don't mind."

"Good idea," said Nick. "Give things time to settle down back at the dormitory before you go back and move out." The older youth went off, his footsteps thudding down the stairs and out of hearing.

Randal stayed behind, staring at the carefully stacked piles of magic books on the table and the floor. The room had never looked this tidy before. He wondered what Nicolas planned to do with the books—give them to the Schola, probably, as Randal had done with his outgrown clothing.

I just don't understand people, thought Randal.

He dropped his head into his hands. *Gaimar has a wizard's power at his fingertips, and all he does is play games. And Nick . . . Nick makes Gaimar look like nothing, and he's giving it up to be an ordinary carpenter.*

And then there's me. Magic's the only thing I want, and like Gaimar said, I can't even light a candle.

But Madoc had said that Randal might have the makings of a wizard. And the northerner wouldn't have lied to him—wouldn't have brought him on the long journey from Doun to Tarnsberg, and taught him reading and writing along the way, if he didn't think Randal had a chance.

A chance. Only a chance. That doesn't mean I'll ever get

there. Maybe I'll just fight with it for years until I've been around the Schola even longer than Nick . . . and then give it up to go tend sheep or something.

The thought frightened Randal. Suddenly, he felt that he had to know—or if certainty was impossible, he needed at least some hint that his struggle wouldn't always remain fruitless. He thought of the vision he'd seen in Madoc's scrying bowl back at Doun and the dream that had followed.

For a while after that, he remembered, everything had seemed so clear. Now, slowly, another idea came to him. He resisted at first, but the thought grew steadily stronger.

Maybe if I try again, I can learn more.

He stood up and went over to the pewter mug and pitcher that stood together on the table. Nick usually kept the pitcher full of water from the kitchen downstairs. Randal looked, and saw that the pitcher hadn't yet been emptied for packing.

Good, he thought, and poured some water into the mug.

He carried the mug back to the table and stood looking down at the surface of the water. First- and second-year apprentices didn't study scrying in their classes, but Randal had heard the masters and the senior apprentices talking about how it was done, and he clearly recalled his own experience earlier at Castle Doun.

First, he would need a focus of some sort, an object on which to fix his concentration. Randal scrabbled around in his belt pouch and pulled out his lump of rock crystal. As Madoc had done long before, he held the crystal out over the water in the bowl, and began to chant in the Old Tongue.

By now, he'd learned enough at the Schola to know that the words were a spell to clear the seer's mind of distractions. *Forget them all,* he thought as the chant went on. *Forget Gaimar, Nicolas, and Lys, forget examinations and failure, forget even wizardry itself. . . . If there's anything for me to see, let it come to me now. . . .*

And then he waited.

Slowly, the air in the stuffy attic room grew cold and the water in the bowl darkened. At last, a spot of color appeared in the water's depths: green, an ugly grayish green like the horizon before a storm. The color spread and filled the mug from lip to lip.

Then Randal saw an empty plain, with gray-green clouds roiling overhead. A young man stood in the center of the flat, dead ground. The black tatters of his apprentice's robe whipped around him in the rising wind.

That's me, thought Randal. As he recognized himself, another spot of green appeared in the iron-hard ground—a healthy, living green this time; the first sprouts of a small plant pushing out of the cracked, bare dirt.

It can't grow much bigger, Randal thought. *Its roots must be choked.*

The youth in the vision turned and pulled something out of the packed earth behind him.

A sword, thought Randal. And then, *My sword. The one my father gave me. The one I threw away.*

The Randal of the vision took the sword and used

it like a spade to turn the dry soil around the small, struggling plant. By dint of great effort, he broke up one clod of dirt, and then another. The plant put out another shoot.

Then the plant began to grow faster and faster, putting out leaf after leaf as Randal freed it from the imprisoning soil. Thunder rolled overhead, and the storm broke. Heavy rain poured down, soaking into the dry ground where Randal had turned it, plastering his black robe to his body. The sword in his hand began to shift and change until he held not a weapon but a wizard's staff.

The wind howled across the empty plain. He raised the staff over his head, and all around him green plants sprang forth from the earth and spread to cover the barren ground. The gray clouds broke and drifted away, uncovering a sapphire-blue sky. The air grew soft and warm, and the field of new green blossomed in the sudden sunshine.

Randal felt tired after his labors. He lay down among the flowers, and slept. . . .

He awoke to a pounding headache and a darkened room. Voices murmured back and forth just out of his hearing range, and someone was putting a cool, damp cloth on his forehead.

"What . . . ?" he murmured.

"He's awake," somebody said. The voice was soft, and the speaker wasn't far away—Lys, from the tone and the Southlands accent. Randal looked and saw the player-girl standing by the head of the cot, a damp rag in her hand.

"About time," said another, deeper voice.

81

"Nick?" asked Randal. He turned his head a little and saw the brown-bearded apprentice—*former apprentice,* he reminded himself—regarding him anxiously.

"That's right," said Nick. "It's me. We came back from the Grinning Gryphon and found you out cold on the floor. Just what did you think you were doing, anyway?"

Randal closed his eyes again. "Looking at the future."

"Without somebody standing by?" Nick sounded almost angry. "You poured enough energy into that scrying to knock out ten wizards, never mind a half-baked apprentice, and you're lucky we got here when we did."

"Thanks," said Randal wearily. *At least now I know I have the power to call on,* he thought. *I ought to be happy about that.* But right now, he was too wrung out by the experience to feel anything but exhaustion.

"I'll try not do it again," he said.

"You'd better not," said Nick. "If you don't stay alive, how on earth am I going to go around in my old age telling people that I knew you when?"

Lys broke in before Randal could answer. "What did you see?" she asked. "You did see the future, didn't you?"

"Yes," said Randal. He felt himself drifting back to sleep again, exhausted by the efforts he had put forth in his vision. "I have to go on," he murmured. "I have to free my magic before the storm clouds break."

VII.
One More Chance

RANDAL'S ATTEMPT AT scrying had come close to killing him, but the near disaster had brought good results as well. With his renewed certainty about the course of his own future, he no longer had the sensation of beating his head against some kind of wall between him and his magic. If he wasn't yet working on the level of the other second-year apprentices, his skills did at least improve enough to keep him from feeling like the class dunce.

Moving out of the dormitory and into Nick's old room also helped. Without the distraction of other apprentices working and talking around him day and night, he had more free time for study—even after doing chores around the carpentry shop to pay his keep. Best of all, he no longer had to put up with Gaimar's irritating presence.

His control of the minor magics grew surer as he used them more often. Calling up a cold-flame reading light took only his own efforts, while candles and lamp oil cost money; after a week or so of halting his studies at sundown, he learned to summon the light and hold it steady while he worked on something else. Unlike the wizards and apprentices of the Schola who thought nothing of working late into the night, the carpenter closed up his shop well before dark—so Randal learned the spells of locking and unlocking in order to come and go as he pleased.

When the day for his second-year examinations came around, Randal felt nervous but—for the first time in months—somewhat hopeful. He woke up early in the morning, put on clean clothes and his apprentice's gown, and walked through the quiet streets to the Schola. This time the doors of the grand hall opened for him at once, and he climbed the stairs to the library alone.

When I came here, he thought as he entered the great chamber filled from floor to ceiling with scrolls and books, *I didn't even know what to call a room like this.*

This time, five master wizards awaited him, seated in a row on the far side of the long table. Mistress Pullen, one of the Regents who had admitted him, sat at the center of the row, flanked by Masters Tarn and Crannach. Once again the young, fair-haired Master Laerg sat at one end of the table . . . and at the other end, his master's robe draped carelessly over the chair back, sat Madoc the Wayfarer.

It's good to see him here, thought Randal. *I hope.* The northern wizard might be a friend, but Randal didn't think Madoc was likely to give him special consideration on that account.

Mistress Pullen folded her hands on the polished

tabletop. "Apprentice Randal," she said. "You may begin by summoning the cold flame."

A reading light . . . that's not too hard. Randal concentrated for a moment and called forth the little tongue of blue-white fire to hover in the air just above and behind him.

Pullen nodded. "Now extinguish the candles."

Randal pictured the yellow flames winking out one by one, and murmured under his breath the spell-words that would channel his will into action. The candles went out, leaving behind only a thin trail of smoke.

The wizards looked at one another. Randal concentrated on keeping the cold flame burning. Then Mistress Pullen said, "Very well, Apprentice . . . now light the candles again."

That was harder. By the time the beeswax candles burned in the branched candlesticks once again, Randal could feel cold drops of sweat trickling down his forehead and the back of his neck.

The questions went on and on. Make the table look like a flat rock. Explain why creating an illusion is not, in fact, the same as telling a lie. Give five basic uses for a magic circle. Draw a simple circle. Activate it. Close it down.

By the time Randal's examination ended, the yellow light of midday streamed through the high windows of the library. He had no idea whether he had done well or poorly, and was almost too tired to care. He felt bruised and exhausted, as though he had spent the time in sword practice with Sir Palamon back at Doun.

"You are dismissed, Apprentice," said Mistress Pullen. "You may wait outside until we summon you again."

Randal left the library. He didn't get far, though, before discovering that the long examination had tired him even more than he thought. As soon as the library door shut behind him, his knees buckled and he had to lean back against the wall for support.

Maybe I should wait here, he thought.

He slid down the polished wood to sit on the floor. For a while he sat there without moving or thinking. Then, slowly, he became aware that he could hear the voices of the five wizards inside the library.

They're talking about me right now, he realized. *I shouldn't be eavesdropping.*

Just the same, he didn't get up and move farther down the stairs. Mistress Pullen's clear, precise tones came through the crack between the door and the frame: " . . . insufficient control for a second-year apprentice, and his technique is crude at best. I'm inclined to recommend dismissal."

Dismissal. Randal bit his lower lip hard. *She means she wants to fail me and throw me out.*

"I beg to differ, Mistress Pullen." Randal recognized Crannach's guttural accent. "What you say is true—but you can't say you haven't noticed the boy's potential. You saw him put out those candles without summoning either wind or water."

"Raw strength does no good without technique to channel it." That was Master Tarn—Randal knew the younger master's voice well from two years of unhappy class meetings. "And his grasp of theory is shaky. We can't afford to make a wizard who doesn't understand why and how a thing is done. I vote for dismissal."

"And I say the Schola can't afford to turn him loose half-trained." Madoc's northern accent was always unmistakable. "Not every student comes here knowing how to learn."

Randal heard a deep chuckle from Crannach. "That's true—I remember a master wizard who showed up on our doorstep barely able to do anything besides tell bad jokes and curse in his own barbarous dialect."

Madoc said something in a language Randal didn't understand, waited for Crannach's answering laughter to subside, and went on in the language of Brecelande. "For some things, experience is the best teacher. I say give the boy time."

"Then we have two votes for retention," said Mistress Pullen, "and two for dismissal. Master Laerg, you haven't spoken yet. . . . How do you vote?"

There was a long pause. Outside the door, Randal held his breath. Then he heard the fair-haired wizard's smooth, almost silky voice. "Odd as it may seem to the rest of you, for once I find myself agreeing with Master Madoc. The boy has too much potential to throw away. I recommend we keep him here on probation. We'll test him again in a few months' time."

Randal let out his breath in a long, explosive sigh of relief. He'd passed . . . even if just barely.

*   *   *

87

Later that day, Randal made a point of paying a visit to the Grinning Gryphon in time to hear Lys perform for the afternoon crowd. The young player had lost her thin and starving look, although she still could pass for a boy in her short tunic. The audience at the tavern—being mostly wizards, and accustomed to looking past the surfaces of things— probably realized that they were listening to a girl, but nobody seemed to care.

The applause and the coins they tossed into the dish in front of her kept her singing until finally she stopped and held up a hand. "Please," she said. "Leave me some voice for tomorrow."

Amid the good-natured comments of the crowd, the player-girl left her place at the center of the room and joined Randal at a corner table. "Good news?" she asked as she sat down next to him.

He nodded, and felt his face break into a smile. "I passed."

"That's wonderful!" Lys exclaimed, and hugged him.

"Well . . . it's not that wonderful," he admitted. "I'm on probation, as usual."

"What's 'probation' mean around here?" she asked.

"It means they examine me again in a few months," said Randal. "If I'm not making enough progress, they throw me out."

"They won't throw you out," said a familiar voice.

Randal gave a start. He looked around and saw Madoc seated at the next table. The master wizard had a tankard in front of him and looked like he'd been sitting there in comfort for some time.

"They won't?" asked Randal. "How can you be sure?"

"Because," said the wizard, "Master Crannach and I have wagered our reputations on it."

"I see," said Randal. He wondered why Madoc hadn't mentioned Master Laerg. But asking about the third vote against dismissal would mean admitting that he'd listened outside the library door. Randal decided to let the matter drop. "I'll try not to disappoint you."

"Continue to make progress," said Madoc, "and you won't."

The wizard turned to Lys, who was sitting quietly, listening to the conversation. "I thought I knew all the notable bards in Brecelande," he said, "but my ears tell me I was wrong."

Lys reddened a little. "I'm only an entertainer, Master Wizard, and not a bard—and as much of an outlander in Brecelande as you are."

"Whatever you call yourself," said Madoc, "and wherever you come from, you have the gift."

The player-girl lowered her head, and Randal saw her fingers tighten on the neck of her lute. "I sing for my supper as best I can. And speaking of supper, I must be gone—mine's cooling in the kitchen this very minute."

She slipped off through the crowd. Randal looked back at Madoc. "I think you scared her a little."

"Perhaps," said Madoc. "Not every strolling player is fit to be called a bard—and not all would wish to be one." He leaned back against the wall with a sigh. "Among my people, to be a bard is a notable thing."

"Better than being a wizard?" asked Randal, remembering Crannach's remarks to Madoc that morning.

"The northlands have little use for wizardry," Madoc told him. "They believe in its reality and they understand its power, but they can't see why they should respect it on that account. Your friends back at Doun aren't any different—just more polite."

Randal thought of Sir Palamon, who had called the wizard "Master Madoc" from their first meeting, and of Lord Alyen, who had set Madoc in a place of honor at the high table. "I don't understand."

"They fear us," said Madoc. "They trust what they see and feel, and they prefer their enemies to stand and fight them face to face. But we can change the look and texture of the world, and we fight among shadows. Why do you think," he asked Randal suddenly, "that wizards are forbidden to use knightly weapons?"

Randal shook his head. "I don't know."

"You mean the masters at the Schola have given you so many reasons you can't choose among all of them," said Madoc. "Well, let me give you another one to think about: It's a rule meant to remind both us and people like your uncle that a true wizard has no business seeking worldly power."

The wizard finished off the contents of his tankard and stood up. "It's time I was off," he said.

"You're going?" asked Randal. "But you just got here."

"Of all the cities in Brecelande," said Madoc, "Tarnsberg is without doubt the best and the fairest. But as any of the masters here will tell you, I'm not much of a man for staying long in one place."

"When will you be back again?"

Madoc shrugged. "Who knows? Mind your studies, and you'll do well enough on your own."

The wizard made his way out the door, leaving Randal sitting by himself at the table. After a while, the apprentice paid for his own mug of cider and headed home.

A few days later, Randal was working alone in the Schola library. Since passing his examinations he'd taken to studying there, as well as in his room above the carpentry shop. In both places he could practice his spells and charms without a running commentary from other apprentices—especially from Gaimar—and in the library he could always find a book or a scroll when he needed one.

Today he was practicing magic circles. His lips moved in a magical verse from the Old Tongue, while with the tip of his index finger he inscribed a circle on the dark wood of the tabletop. Then, still using the tip of his finger as a marker, he added the basic symbols at north, south, east, and west. He spoke a few more words in the Old Tongue—and the tiny circle began to glow.

Randal relaxed. The process had never gone so smoothly before. Now if he could only manage to activate a full-sized circle with the same ease . . .

"Excellent work."

Randal started. He turned and saw Master Laerg standing a few paces behind him. The fair-haired young master wizard wore his Schola robes over a long tunic of deep purple velvet, making Randal even more conscious than usual of his own threadbare hand-me-downs.

Laerg's expression, however, was one of interest as he inspected Randal's practice circle. "I see that you've already made progress since your examination."

"Thank you, sir," said Randal. He waited curiously to hear what the master wizard would say next, but the question, when it came, surprised him.

"Have you given any thought to finding a tutor for your third-year studies?"

Randal shook his head. He'd never bothered to worry about finding an individual master willing to give him further instruction beyond the basic first- and second-year classes. There seemed to be no point to it while he was half expecting to find himself thrown out of the Schola after the second-year examination.

And now—if Madoc were here, the choice would be easy. But the northerner was out on the road again, and who knew when he would return?

"Perhaps Master Crannach . . ." Randal began.

"He already has more apprentices than he can do justice to," said Laerg. "I'm afraid that he might inadvertently stunt a student with your potential."

Randal forgot about politeness. "What potential?" he asked bitterly. "I'm barely starting to learn stuff most of the other apprentices picked up inside the first six months."

"I know," said Laerg. "It's your very potential that gets in the way when you try to work the simple magics. Consider those candles you extinguished for the examination."

"I remember them," said Randal. *I remember how I stood there sweating after I finally did something everybody else does with a wave of the hand.* "What about the candles?" he asked.

"Most students," said Laerg, "will blow out the candles with a gust of wind—easy, inconspicuous, and direct. The preferred answer, in fact. A few students will choose to summon up a rain shower or a heavy mist, and drown the flames in water. Almost never do we see a student who is able to do what you did: to draw heat out of the candles by the power of will."

So that's how I did it, thought Randal. *The hard way, as usual.* "That's the wrong answer?"

"Yes," said Laerg, "and no. No, because of the sheer power it demonstrates, and yes, because the student cannot control that same power."

Randal thought for a minute. It was good to hear a master wizard tell him to his face that he had power; even Madoc had never been as direct as that. But the knowledge didn't help with his current problem.

"If Master Crannach can't take me as a student, who will?"

"I can," said Laerg. He reached into a pocket of his robe and pulled out a small, gnarled object Ran-

93

dal recognized as a peach pit. He handed the pit to Randal. "Plant this."

Randal blinked. "In what?"

"Whatever pleases you," said Laerg. "Here, perhaps." The master wizard pointed a finger at the table and spoke a phrase in the Old Tongue. The heavy wood shifted and changed, becoming a wooden tub filled with dirt.

The air in the library grew cold as the table changed, and Randal knew that this was no illusion—the table had truly become what it appeared to be. Laerg nodded at him, and Randal shoved the peach pit down into the soft humus.

"Now," said Master Laerg, "make it grow."

Randal shook his head. "I can't—I've never studied advanced spells like that."

"Nevertheless, you can do it. Just as you extinguished the candles." Laerg's voice was persuasive, but firm. "Picture the seed opening, and sending forth its sprouts . . . speak the words for channeling your will into action. . . . "

Randal did as he was told. He felt the force of the spell building up within him, so strong and unwieldy that it threatened to slip away from him and dissolve before he could use it. Then he heard Laerg's voice speaking the words of channeling again, and the spell steadied. A sprout of green showed above the dirt in the wooden tub.

The sprout grew, put forth leaves, stretched out first into a sapling, and then into a flowering tree. Its topmost limbs brushed the high ceiling of the library. In another moment, all the flowers fell onto

the dirt, and golden peaches swelled on the tree's leafy branches.

"You can pick one, if you like," said Laerg.

Randal plucked a ripe peach from the nearest limb. The fruit felt full and heavy, and its plush yellow skin was sticky with oozings of juice. As he watched, still holding the peach, the tree dropped its leaves. Within seconds, it stood withered and barren in the tub of dirt.

Laerg spoke a few words in the Old Tongue. Once more Randal felt the air grow chilly around him, and the bare tree again became a table of polished wood.

"Come to my study tomorrow at noon," said Laerg, "for your first lesson."

The master wizard strode out of the library, his black robe swirling around his ankles. Randal stayed behind, gazing at the ripe peach in his hand, half-afraid to taste it.

VIII.
Sword and Circle

WINTER CAME TO Tarnsberg with frost, snow, and clear starry nights. Then the snows melted, the evenings lengthened, and the warm air of early spring blew between the buildings.

Every day Randal went to Laerg's study for instruction in the higher arts of wizardry—the construction of magic circles, the creation of complex illusions, the control of light and flame. His studies progressed well. With the master wizard to guide him and steady his control when the power he'd brought to a spell threatened to slip away, Randal learned faster than ever before.

Today, the casement windows of Laerg's study were open and the velvet curtains were drawn, letting in the spring breezes and the late-afternoon sunlight. Randal sat on a low wooden stool, listening to the master wizard discourse on the summoning of elementals.

"You will find these methods useful in dealing with spirits of earth, air, fire, and water."

"These spirits—they aren't demons, are they?" asked Randal.

In the six months he'd been studying with Master Laerg, he'd learned a great deal of magical theory. Until now, though, the lessons hadn't touched on the summoning of elementals and other spirits. The Schola didn't forbid such spells, but only the most powerful wizards dared to work them—summonings were among the most dangerous of magics, both to the wizard and to anybody else who might be nearby.

Laerg shook his head to Randal's question. "Demons," said the master wizard, "live on planes other than this earthly one of ours. Elementals are quite the opposite—they are firmly bound to the physical world, even though they are not part of it. Therefore, summoning them is fairly simple. Even an apprentice can do it, if properly instructed."

"I see," said Randal. He had an idea what today's project was going to be, and he wasn't certain that he liked it. *I haven't got any use for an elemental even if I can catch one,* he thought. *But I suppose it's good to know how.*

"We will begin," Laerg told him, "by constructing a magic circle of suitable strength. Proceed, please."

Randal stood. An ebony wand lay on the wizard's desk. Randal picked up the wand, and then paused.

"What kind of elemental?" he asked. "And how big?"

"Only a fire elemental of the lowest rank," said

Laerg. "You don't need a circle more than an ell across."

Randal took the ebony wand and used it to inscribe a circle about three hand's-lengths in diameter on the floor of the study. *That's an ell, more or less,* he told himself. *Now for the symbols.*

He added the markings at the four directions and drew between them the glyphs representing the four elements as Laerg had just listed them: earth, air, fire, and water. Then he stepped back from his handiwork and turned to the master wizard for more instructions.

Laerg gave the circle a quick glance and nodded. "Excellent work, so far."

He looked at Randal for a moment, as if appraising him, and then went on. "One more thing, before you begin the summoning: Go to that chest in the corner, and open it. Take out what you find there."

Randal went over to the large, iron-bound chest and lifted the heavy lid. Inside, he found a layer of folded robes and tunics in different shades of heavy velvet—and lying on top of them, something long and thin, wrapped in red silk. He reached in and took hold of the silk-wrapped object.

As soon as he touched it, he knew what it was. His hands shook a little as he freed the sword from its silken bindings—it had been almost three years since he had touched any sort of weapon, let alone a weapon such as this. The thin wire wrapped around the hilt was pure gold, a star ruby winked at him from the pommel, and the blade had the watermark pattern of the finest Southlands steel.

Randal lifted the sword, and found that his hand and wrist still knew the proper way to grasp the weapon and hold it steady.

But what kind of wizardry uses a sword? he wondered.

Behind him, as if in answer, he heard Laerg's voice, saying, "In summoning elementals, as in summoning demons and the greater spirits, the use of proper symbolism is all-important. Strictly speaking, the power and authority embodied in the ceremonial blade are not required when dealing with such petty powers. A wand would be quite sufficient. Only those who dare to summon the most powerful spirits must lock them with steel. But if you are to learn those most mighty magics, you must practice first at a lower level with the tools of the higher. Hence, as you see, the bladed weapon."

Randal looked at the sunlight winking off the unblemished steel—no flaws, no thin spots from the whetstone. *This is no knight's weapon,* he realized. *It's been kept wrapped up ever since it was forged, and never used against anything stronger than air.*

"Now," said Laerg, "place the sword outside the circle, with the ruby in the pommel pointing to the west. Then activate the circle and repeat the words of summoning."

Randal laid down the sword as Laerg had instructed. Then he took up the wand again, and extended it over the circle. At a whispered phrase in the Old Tongue, the circle sprang into glowing life.

Now for the words of summoning. Randal licked his lips nervously as he went over the incantation in his mind. Even an apprentice wizard knew the chief danger of summoning—one slip of the tongue, one break in the circle, and the wizard might become a victim of the forces he'd tried to master.

But Randal's months of study had given him confidence, and the words of the spell flowed into his mind without flaw or hesitation. He drew a deep breath, and began to speak.

As always when he tried to work the higher-level magics, Randal felt his power build up and then start to fade away. Almost without thought, he steadied his control and continued to recite the words of summoning.

"Fiat!" he concluded in the Old Tongue. *Let it be done.*

Something small and orange-colored appeared in the center of the circle: a doll-sized creature made entirely out of flame. It blinked and wavered, as if the breeze coming in through the open windows threatened to extinguish it. Then it seemed to get its bearings. Its fiery substance grew brighter and it began to move about as it tested the limits of its prison—stopping short first at one edge of the circle and then the other, leaving little smoking footprints as it went.

The creature halted its restless motion, and Randal knew that it had noticed his presence. He could sense the fire elemental's attention directed at himself, and at the sword that lay just outside the circle's glowing boundary.

. . . you called me . . . The elemental's voice was like a whisper in his mind.

101

"I called you," he agreed aloud.

. . . *what do you want me to do? . . .*

"Want?" asked Randal. "Nothing."

. . . *but you summoned me . . .* The faint mind-voice of the elemental sounded frustrated and afraid. . . . *command me, or I cannot go back! . . .*

"I don't want to command you to do anything," said Randal.

. . . *but you must! . . .* The elemental blazed up with a bright and angry light, pushing hard against the boundaries of the circle in all directions at once. . . . *you must! . . .*

Randal frowned, thinking. "Then I command you to give me your name, and come once more when I call you."

The elemental's blaze died back down to doll size once again. . . . *my name is Flashfire. . . . call me once more, and I will come to serve you. . . .*

"Good," said Randal. "You can go now. I release you."

The elemental winked out like a torch in a high wind. Randal waited a few seconds to be certain it was truly gone, and then shut down the circle.

"Now," said Laerg when the last trace of the circle had been erased and the sword had been returned to its silk wrappings, "you see how simple such a summoning really is."

Randal gave a reluctant nod. For all the power that it required, the spell *had* been a simple one—in fact, it had felt almost *too* simple for something that could hold a fire spirit. Nor had that been all. . . .

"I still don't understand the reason for using the sword," he admitted to Laerg. "I've read about summoning-spells before, and none of the books mentioned weapons."

"Not everything," said Laerg, "can be safely entrusted to a written page, where any fool can read it. The highest magics have always been passed down from teacher to student by the spoken word alone. And some things I have discovered for myself, going beyond the limits set by dead tradition."

"Oh," said Randal. "But what about the sword?"

For a moment, Laerg seemed annoyed. Then the shadow left the master wizard's handsome features and he went on in his smooth, lecturer's voice. "As I said before, the sword is only a symbol: in this case, a symbol of power. Elementals and similar spirits, especially those inhabiting other planes of existence, have limited intelligence, and understand very little else. One must speak to them," the master wizard concluded, "in ways that they will understand."

Randal nodded slowly. Laerg's words made sense, but something about the summoning still bothered him—he couldn't rid himself of the memory of the fire elemental pacing about the circle like a wild creature penned in a cage.

He brooded about it for the rest of the afternoon and finally headed at dusk for the Grinning Gryphon. Lys would be performing there during the dinner hour, and he could talk with her afterward. With Nick gone and Madoc on the road, he had no other close friends in Tarnsberg.

Night had fallen by the time he reached the inn, and the common room was packed with customers. Lys was singing, her clear alto voice rising above the rippling notes of the lute. Randal bought himself a mug of cider and settled back in his usual corner to wait until she had finished.

> "Lie there, lie there, you false sir knight,
>   Lie there and let me be.
> It's seven maids that you have drowned,
>   But the eighth one has drowned thee."

The last notes of the old ballad died away. The patrons of the Grinning Gryphon no doubt already knew the tale of the murderous lover and the valiant damsel who at last brought him to defeat, but they cheered Lys to the rafters nonetheless. She swept the crowd a parting bow, tossed her mop of black curls back out of her eyes, and made her way through the tables to join Randal.

"Playing for wizards is going to spoil me for a real audience," she observed as she took her seat. "You'd think they'd never heard music before."

"They appreciate skill," said Randal. "In everything." He fell silent again, remembering the music that Madoc had called out of the air that evening in Castle Doun so long ago.

He set the mug of cider down on the table and called up a miniature image of the shimmering tree of light the master wizard had created to go with his music. But the image fragmented almost as soon as he brought it into being, leaving only a brief golden haze in the air above the table. He dropped his hand back down into his lap and sighed.

Lys had been watching the little illusion as it grew and faded; now she gave him a curious look. "What's wrong?" she asked. "For somebody who could barely light a candle six months ago, you're doing pretty well."

"I suppose so," said Randal. "But—"

He sighed again, and then began telling Lys about that afternoon's lesson with Master Laerg. He described the fire elemental, pushing and testing the bounds of its magical prison. "All it wanted was to get away, but it had to *beg* me to give it an order first!"

"A lot of people," observed Lys with a wry smile, "would enjoy doing something like that."

"Well, I didn't," said Randal. "And if that's what the higher magic is all about, then I'm not sure I want anything to do with it."

Hearing himself say the words aloud startled him, but even as he spoke he realized that they were true. *What I'm learning isn't what I wanted to learn.*

"Maybe you should talk to Master Madoc the next time he's in town," said Lys. "He didn't look like somebody who'd enjoy making fireflies jump through hoops."

Randal smiled in spite of his depression. "No. He isn't. But it could be months before he shows up again. And what do I do with myself in the meantime?"

She tilted her head and looked closely at him. "Go home and get some sleep. You look tired all the time these days. Maybe Master Laerg isn't the right teacher for you, after all."

Randal thought about her words as he walked back to the attic room above the carpentry shop, but his mood still troubled him as he prepared himself for bed. He lay awake for a long time, watching a beam of moonlight move across the floor and listening to the night sounds of the city.

At last he slept—deeply at first, and then he dreamed.

In his dream, he walked through the streets of Tarnsberg, as he had on the day he first arrived. He came to the open door of the Grinning Gryphon and went inside. The common room was empty, without even a fire burning on the great hearth; he went on upstairs to the room where he had stayed on first coming to town, and flung the door open without knocking.

Randal strode into the room—and found himself standing under the open sky in the midst of a group of folk, lords and tradesmen and wizards in their robes of mastery. All the people bowed low and stepped away. He saw that he was on the slope of a high hill overlooking Tarnsberg, with the city stretching out below him around its half-moon bay.

The folk who stood with him began to circle around him faster and faster and change their forms until they were nothing more than whirling shadows in the shapes of men and women. A high wind began to blow across the hilltop, howling with a noise like the sound of wild beasts starving in winter.

The crowd of shadows danced around him on the

rising wind, moving closer and then drawing away. He tried to see their faces, but their features remained blurred and indistinct whenever he looked directly at them, no matter how familiar they seemed out of the corner of his eye.

Illusion! he thought, and cried out in the Old Tongue the words that would clear his sight and show him reality.

As the last syllables left his throat, he saw for the first time that the shadowy forms had no faces. Instead, they went masked as they capered about. He reached out an arm toward the nearest dancer, and snatched the mask away—and behind it found only another, blanker mask.

He heard a sound like enormous laughter or the blast of a brazen trumpet, and the dancers parted again to reveal a lighted door opening up on the hillside before him. The light drew him, and he stepped through the open door.

Once again he stood in the streets of Tarnsberg. But the city had changed from the town which Madoc had called the best and the fairest. All the people had vanished, and garbage choked the empty cobblestone streets.

A dark alley spilled out a pile of waste almost at Randal's feet. He drew back from the foul-smelling heap, and then stepped forward again. A book from the Schola library had somehow found a place amid the rubbish. The volume lay open on top of the stinking refuse, the gold leaf and colored inks of the book's illuminated pages shining jewel-bright against the filth and decay.

It shouldn't be lying there, he thought, and picked it up. *It has to go back to the Schola where it belongs.*

But the Schola proved to be as decaying and deserted as the city itself. The library where he had twice been tested stood empty and full of dust, and the air inside had a rotten, moldy taint. Randal went to the nearest shelf and tried to put the book into place among the crumbling, dog-eared volumes.

The book fell off the shelf onto the floor. Randal picked it up, and put it back into place. Again, it fell to the floor.

A third time, Randal shelved the book, and a third time, it fell. The pages opened as it hit the floor.

He picked up the book. This time, when he looked at it, he saw that the pages were written in an unfamiliar script. He looked closer, but could not recognize the language—it was not the speech of Brecelande, nor the Old Tongue, but some language Randal had never seen. He frowned over the strange syllables, trying them out in his mind to hear if they matched any of the other languages he had heard in his time at the Schola: the harsh gutturals of Crannach's native tongue, or Lys's fluid Southlands speech, or the lilting, sibilant language of Madoc's homeland.

Try as he might, the words remained gibberish, and he became oppressed by the feeling that the book held important knowledge, magical secrets that with all the will in the world he could never master. The leather-bound volume became heavy in his hands, and still heavier, until the weight dragged him down to his knees on the dusty, rotting wood of the library floor.

He tried to let go of the book, but he could not. All the while it grew heavier and heavier, and the floorboards creaked and sagged beneath him. At last the floor gave way with a noise of rending wood, and he fell. . . .

Randal awakened.

Once again, he lay on the narrow bed in the room above the carpenter shop. The room was empty, with no friends to help him back from the strange landscape of his dreams. His sheet had tangled itself around his thrashing body during the night, and his skin was slick with sweat. The first light of dawn came in through the attic window.

He felt tired and aching and several years older than the Randal who had gone to bed the night before. Moving slowly, he unwound himself from the knot of sheets and got out of bed. He shivered a little as the cool morning air struck his bare skin.

He went over to the table and washed the sweat off his body with water from the pitcher. When he was clean, he put on his clothes, and over them he draped the black robe of an apprentice wizard.

Then he quietly went down the staircase and out through the shop into the empty street.

IX.
Wizard's Blood

TARNSBERG WAS QUIET in the early morning and not many of its citizens were stirring. But even so, the scene was a long way from the desolation of Randal's dream.

Curls of smoke rose from the city's many stone chimneys, and the early-morning smell of baking bread tickled Randal's nose as he strode through the section of town that housed the bakeries and cookshops. Here and there, the wooden shutters of the shopfronts clattered open, letting out the sound of still-sleepy voices inside. Somewhere a few streets away, a drover shouted cries of encouragement to his draft animals as his heavy oxcart rumbled and thudded over the rough cobblestones.

Randal looked about the streets as if seeing them for the first time. *I understand now why Madoc called the city beautiful,* he thought. *It's not the buildings, the hills, or the ocean . . . it's the* aliveness *of it all.*

"Randal!"

At the sound of Lys's voice, he stopped. The

110

player-girl ran down the street toward him, coming from the direction of the Grinning Gryphon.

"What's going on?" he asked. Lys stayed up late most nights, singing at the Gryphon until closing time, and didn't often stir at this hour of the morning.

"I came to tell you," she said. "Your friend Master Madoc is back in town. He showed up this morning just as Cook was opening up the kitchen."

Madoc's back. Randal hadn't realized until now exactly how much he'd missed the northerner's help and advice. "Tell him I need to talk with him this morning," he told Lys. "I'll be at the Gryphon before noon."

"Why not now?" asked Lys. "He'll probably be finished with breakfast by the time we get there."

Randal shook his head. "I have to go somewhere first."

"At this hour?"

"Before I do anything else," said Randal. "I had a dream last night."

"You had a—oh. Like when you saw the future that time."

"Not quite. I didn't ask for this one." Randal was silent a moment, remembering. "But—you know the stuff I talked about yesterday evening?"

"It's why I came to tell you about Madoc."

Randal smiled at her. "Thanks. But the dream told me at least part of what I needed to know: studying with Master Laerg isn't for me, and I have to tell him so."

Lys looked concerned. "But you ought to have a teacher. You said that yourself."

"Maybe Crannach will take me if he isn't too busy. And there's always Tarn or Issen. And if they won't have me"—Randal shrugged—"then either I'll find someone else or I'll do what I can on my own. But before I can do that, I have to tell Master Laerg."

"Can't it wait until after you talk to Madoc?"

"No," said Randal. "I have to go to Laerg first."

Lys gave him an odd look. "If you say so. I'll see you at the Gryphon after breakfast."

She headed back the way she had come, and Randal continued through the dawn-lit streets toward the Schola. A yawning, bleary-eyed senior apprentice let him in through the main door. Randal made his way through the halls toward the area where the resident masters lived.

Inside the Schola, most of the students and teachers still slept, but a few early risers were already moving about. Randal passed a couple of black-robed apprentices—both new since his time in the dormitory—and stopped to greet Pieter, who had played the doorkeeper for his examination by the Regents.

Pieter had passed his own final examinations, and like Boarin in the dormitory, now wore a master's robe himself. He met Randal with a sleepy version of his usual friendly smile.

"What brings you here so early?" Pieter asked. "I thought apprentices moved out of the dormitory so they could sleep late in the mornings."

"Funny," said Randal, "I thought that was why journeymen became master wizards."

"Not if they plan to hang around the Schola," said Pieter. "Somebody has to get up and cast spells to make sure the kitchen fires get lit and the day's bread rises—and it isn't the senior masters, I can tell you that much. But they're great ones for conjuring until all hours and then not showing their faces until noon."

"Not all of them," said Randal. "Master Laerg does a lot of his work in the early morning."

Pieter looked Randal up and down. "And drags his apprentice in from town to help him, it seems," said the junior master after a moment's consideration. "Well, good luck with today's project. I'm off to wake up the kitchen."

Randal continued on into the section of the Schola that housed the senior resident masters. Laerg had a suite of rooms that included a tower on the corner above the uppermost floor, at the top of a narrow circular staircase. The staircase was cramped and lit only by a single narrow window on each level. As Randal went up the steps, he saw a yellow glow in the dimness ahead—light escaping from under the door of the master wizard's tower chamber.

Good, thought Randal. *I won't have to wake him up to give him the news.*

He knocked on the door.

"Come in!" called Laerg's voice from within the chamber. Randal knew another moment of relief— the master wizard hadn't sounded upset about the disturbance. Often, interruptions during working hours made Laerg irritable and less patient with an apprentice's errors. If the master wizard was in a good mood, taking leave of him would be easier.

Randal gave the door a push. It swung open, and then gently shut behind him as he stepped inside the room. Looking around, Randal saw that the master wizard had indeed been about his conjurations earlier this morning: heavy curtains still covered the casement windows, shutting out all the outside light, and candles set about the corners of the room burned low in their sockets. A faint, smoky haze streaked the air, and the acrid, sweetish smell of incense tickled Randal's nostrils.

More than all that, though, the atmosphere in the room vibrated with the power of the spells that had been cast. Three years ago, Randal would never have perceived the change; six months ago, he wouldn't have understood the source. But his time with Master Laerg had not all been ill spent, even if he had decided to find another teacher; these days he could recognize the traces of a major conjuration.

Laerg sat in his usual chair on the far side of the room. The fair-haired wizard still wore the robes which he donned only for the most important magical occasions: heavy garments of purple velvet embroidered with occult symbols stitched in stiff gold thread. He looked tired and satisfied at the same time—whatever spells he had cast, Randal decided, must have proved difficult but successful. Now Laerg rose from the chair and came forward.

"Good morning, Randal. I've been expecting you."

Randal hesitated. *I didn't decide to come here until half an hour ago.*

Laerg smiled. "If only you could study further, you'd learn that few things are hidden from a master wizard—least of all the impending arrival of an apprentice."

Then he knows why I came here, too, thought Randal. Aloud, he asked, "What do you mean—'if only I could study further'?"

Laerg gestured at the low stool where Randal usually sat during lessons. "Sit down," he invited, "and let me explain."

Randal sat down. Laerg resumed his place in his own chair, and leaned back with the tips of his fingers steepled together.

"The first question that they ask you when you come to the Schola," he said, "is, 'why do you want to be a wizard?' And at the final examination for mastery, the last question they ask you is just the same."

The master magician looked at Randal through half-closed eyes and smiled as if thinking about some private joke. "Why do you want to be a wizard?" he said again. "Nobody's ever given a good answer to that one, as far as the Regents are concerned, and nobody ever will."

Randal, made bold by the master's confidences and by his own decision to seek a new teacher, said, "Maybe nobody knows the right answer, after all."

Laerg laughed softly. "The Regents of the Schola

certainly don't. Power beyond imagining lies in their grasp, and they do nothing with it. The weakest among them would have only to stretch out his hand, and the entire kingdom of Brecelande would fall into it like a ripe peach off the tree.''

A true wizard has no business seeking worldly power. Randal seemed to hear Madoc's voice repeating those words as clearly as he'd spoken them once before in the common room of the Grinning Gryphon.

"I don't think," said Randal aloud, "that the Regents of the Schola want to control the Kingdom of Brecelande, or anyplace else."

"The more fools they," said Laerg. "The kingdom is without a ruler, and sooner or later somebody will take it, whether the Schola approves the deed or not."

"Somebody?" asked Randal. He remembered his dream, with all the shadowy figures bowing down before him, and the Schola in ruins. "Don't you mean, 'some wizard'?"

Laerg smiled at him. "You're not completely hopeless, after all. It's possible I could have kept you with me, but I don't dare risk it, not when Madoc was your first teacher. He and Crannach were right about one thing, at least—you have a great deal of potential power. It's a pity I won't be able to help you bring it to fruition."

"Yes, well . . . that's really what I'm here about," said Randal. "I came to say that I can't be your student any longer."

"You came," said Laerg, "because I summoned you. I do have a use for you, Randal. . . . I'd hoped

116

to delay things until a more fortunate time, but then you started slipping away from me and I decided not to hold off any longer."

Randal nodded slowly. "You summoned me. That explains why I wouldn't wait to talk to Master Madoc before I came here."

"Madoc's in town? Then I've got little time to waste, and I'm glad that you're here with me," said Laerg. "I couldn't let you see him—he might have noticed something. I've never liked your northern friend . . . and he, I regret to say, has never quite trusted me." The fair-haired wizard laughed. "Perhaps he'll realize he was right, before the end."

"Before the end?" All Randal's vague forebodings suddenly congealed into a hard lump in his chest. "What are you planning to do?"

Laerg looked pleased with himself. "Do? I'm going to kill them all, of course."

"You're going to—?" Randal heard his voice threatening to crack on the last word, and stopped. Forcing himself to speak calmly, he asked, "How?"

"With aid from the demonic plane," said Laerg. "I've spent most of the night preparing the gateway, and now the only thing lacking is blood to pay the demons for their help."

Randal felt cold. "If you're planning to kill the whole Schola," he said, "I think the demons will have blood enough."

"By the time they're finished," said Laerg. "But the high lords of the demon kind take their payments in advance—first the blood, and then the slaughter."

Randal knotted his fingers together on his knees, the better to keep his hands from shaking. "I suppose it has to be human blood," he said.

"Naturally," said Laerg. "The demon princes are not mere imps and gremlins that can be bought off with sheep's blood or a flask of oil. They want human blood, and to hire the mightiest of them, only the blood of a wizard will serve."

That explains everything, thought Randal. *Why he picked me for his apprentice and taught me so much, so fast; why he doesn't like Madoc; and why he called me here this morning.*

He sprang to his feet, and the footstool turned over with a thud as he dashed for the door.

Laerg made a casual gesture. The space around Randal sprang to flickering, blue-purple life, and the air before him seemed to solidify as he struck it. The impact threw him backward, and he fell.

Randal struggled to his feet.

At the base of the invisible barrier glowed a magic circle big enough to take in almost the whole room. Laerg's chair stood outside the circle, and the smoldering candles surrounded it. Signs and symbols shone with pale blue light at the four points of the compass. From his readings in the Schola library, Randal recognized the names of demon lords so powerful that even master wizards seldom dared speak the syllables out loud.

I'm trapped, he thought. In despair, he tried the only spell he knew that might help, a simple charm of opening that he'd learned after old John Carpenter had locked the shop doors early for three nights in a row.

"It won't do any good," said Laerg. "I have you now, apprentice—magic and all."

He made another gesture, and the candles flared up again, filling the room with hazy orange light. By their glow, Randal saw what he hadn't seen before, or what he had been kept from seeing while he talked with Laerg. A small, stubby-legged copper cauldron stood just outside the circle's luminous boundary, and across the mouth of the cauldron lay the great gold-hilted sword. The ruby in its pommel shone in the candlelight like a drop of blood.

Laerg rose to his feet and stood over the cauldron. Lifting his arms and spreading them wide, he began to chant aloud in the Old Tongue, calling on the demon lords by name and speaking the words that, once they had taken the blood he offered, would bind them to work his will and do him no harm.

"Principes demonorum invoco. . . ."

The resounding words seemed to thunder in the small chamber. Randal stood in the center of the circle, listening to the roll call of the lords of darkness. The walls of the room began to glow as the incantation went on. Randal knew they soon would collapse under the pressure from the demonic plane. Then the demon princes would appear and demand their payment—the blood of a wizard.

His blood.

Randal bit back a cry of fear. Far away in the back of his head, he seemed to hear Sir Palamon, the master-at-arms of Castle Doun. *Never panic, boy. It only keeps you from thinking.*

He clenched his fists. *But what else can I do?* he demanded of that long-ago voice. *He's a master wizard, and I'm only an apprentice—and he already controls the little magic I know.*

Once again, he seemed to hear Sir Palamon's voice. *The day may come when you won't have your shield, and you won't have your armor, and you won't have your friends beside you, but you'll have your sword and your skill. Those will always be with you.*

Randal remembered. He looked again at the gold-hilted sword lying across the copper cauldron—just outside the circle, and therefore beyond his reach.

"Venite, venite, principes demonorum . . . " Laerg chanted.

Randal began to fall into despair once more, and then another memory struck him—the sound of his own voice this time, speaking to a small, flickering presence too weak to escape his reluctant control. *I command you to give me your name, and come once more when I call you.*

"Flashfire," he murmured aloud under the vocal thunder of Laerg's incantation.

A light appeared in the far corner of the room, outside the orange glow of the candles and the eldritch lights of the magic circle. The faint voice of the fire elemental whispered again in Randal's mind.

. . . you called me, and I am here . . . do you have a command for me, that I may go? . . .

Randal tried to keep his own speech at the level of that unvoiced murmur. *Only one thing, Flashfire, and then you can be gone. Do you see the sword lying across the cauldron?*

The fiery creature flickered and rose up again. *. . . bad thing. I see it. . . .*

Good, said Randal. He paused. What he was contemplating, once done, could never be undone—and if he didn't die here and now, he would have to live forever after with the consequences. One second more he hesitated, and then spoke again to the elemental. *Only push the sword into the circle, and you may go.*

The spark of light disappeared from its place in the corner and reappeared, hovering over the sword and cauldron. Laerg chanted on.

Now! thought Randal, and Flashfire's spark of light winked out as the sword slid free. The metal scraped along the rim of the cauldron, and then the blade clattered onto the floor. The cauldron tipped and fell over with a crash.

Now the tip of the blade lay inside the boundary of the magic circle.

Laerg stopped chanting. Before the master wizard could turn toward him, Randal made a grab for the sword, catching it by the tip and dragging it into the circle. The blade might have been unused, but it was sharp enough all the same; he felt the edge cutting into his palm.

Laerg raised a hand, and his lips moved. Randal could hear the master wizard's voice starting in on the first syllables of a new spell—something to stun an enemy or make him immobile.

Randal closed his bleeding hand around the grip of the sword. He could see where the point would have to end up—on the other side of the master wizard's body. He brought the weapon up into guard position behind his back. Then he swung the blade, as if cutting at Laerg's leg. At the last moment, he straightened his arm and stepped forward with his rear foot, turning his thrust into a lunge. The blade went true. Randal's hand fetched up against the magic circle, but the unliving blade penetrated where his body could not.

The sharp steel took Laerg in the abdomen, pinning the master wizard to the chamber wall. Then, as part of the same movement, Randal took a step back, wrenching the sword free. He came to the guard position with the blade behind his back, ready to strike again.

Laerg looked surprised. His eyes met Randal's. "How odd," he said. "I never thought of a wizard using a sword that way."

And then the master wizard collapsed, bleeding, across the edge of the magic circle.

Randal felt the circle break. The gold-hilted sword weighed heavily in his hand. He remembered what Mistress Pullen had said on the day the Regents admitted him to the Schola: *You must never attack or defend with sword or dagger or any knightly weapon. Their use is forbidden to practitioners of the mystic arts.*

But he didn't have time to reflect on what he had done. The walls opened, and a host of twisted, mis-

122

shapen things came boiling into the room: demons called from their own plane by Laerg's conjurings, ready to seal their bargain by drinking a wizard's blood.

X.

The Open Gate

RANDAL CALLED FIRE out of the air, as Gaimar had done during their fight in the dormitory. He threw the globe of flame at the nearest demon. The creature licked up the fire with one flick of its tongue, and laughed at him.

I'm going to die, thought Randal. If the demon lords had enough power to destroy an entire Schola full of master wizards, then the magic of one half-taught apprentice wasn't going to stop them.

Now the demons were twisting into the room, coming through a narrow crack in the reality of space. Watching the demons enter, Randal suddenly realized that they had to squeeze through the gap. Laerg had never fully completed the spell of portal opening.

Maybe there's a chance after all.

Randal lifted his hand and called out the spell of general protection. He followed that up with a charm against nightmares, one that his old nurse had taught him back before he had even left his father's household. *Whatever it does, it can't hurt.*

But he knew that he had to distract the demons from the pool of red fluid spreading out from under Laerg's body. At least if they tried for Randal, they would have a fight. A short fight, he admitted to himself, but a good one.

"If you want a wizard's blood," he shouted at the advancing demons, "then come fight me for mine!"

He glanced down just in time to see a demon lunging for the blood that dripped freely from his wounded hand. He pulled his arm back out of range and tried to call up a lightning bolt—something he had never attempted before.

He felt the power of the spell building within him, then felt it waver and threaten to dissipate before he could use it.

I'm not an apprentice, he thought, and felt a surge of anger at the realization. *I'm a wizard! Laerg made me one, so that my blood would be worth the selling.*

With an extraordinary effort of will, Randal steadied the spell. He launched the bolt at the demon who had tried to lap his blood. The force of the strike hitting so near singed his own hair. Thunder came booming back, and the demon split in two.

At the same moment, the door of the tower chamber burst inward with a noise that dwarfed the thunder. Madoc the Wayfarer stood in the gap, a brilliant light shining at his back. The hot wind from the demonic plane blew his dark hair back from his stern face. He raised his staff over his head and shouted words of power.

The demons wavered. They looked away from Randal to this new threat. The northern wizard

lifted his empty hand. A jet of flame flew across the room, and the nearest demon staggered backward.

On the other side of the chamber, Randal stood over Laerg's body. Randal's slashed hand throbbed where he gripped the sword. Beyond him, something misshapen was trying to force its way through the crack between the planes.

Madoc shouted a command in the Old Tongue. The northerner strode forward into the room, and the demons fell back before him. But his foes were mighty lords on their own plane of existence, and they were far from beaten. Instead of fleeing, they pressed closer to where Randal stood, sword in hand, over the blood-soaked form of Master Laerg.

They need to drink the blood before they can gain their full power, thought Randal, suddenly understanding. *A circle . . . Maybe that will keep them away from the blood.*

Using the blade as if it were a wand, he sketched a magic circle around the crumpled corpse. The monstrosities around him howled, but he set his teeth and went on. For this moment, at least, he was a wizard, and all the horrors of the demonic plane could not keep him from finishing his task.

The blue-white line of the protective circle flashed into existence, and Randal recalled Laerg's words of the day before: *Lock them with steel.*

He laid the blade down with the pommel to the west, and then turned back to the fight.

Madoc advanced still farther into the room. The bright light, almost too strong to look at, shone behind him. Two other figures stepped out of the glare and into the chamber. Randal recognized Master Crannach and Mistress Pullen.

Mistress Pullen sang out a phrase, and spears of rainbow light flew from her. Whenever they touched a demon's flesh, that demon began to melt and dissolve. Master Crannach shouted a few words in his deep voice and pointed at another of the demons. The scaly creature exploded into fragments.

Randal tried to call up another lightning bolt, but the strength that had flooded him before was gone, used up in the casting of the circle.

A demon stooped over him, long fangs snapping for his throat. Randal cast a fireball. It was a pale thing, even compared to the one that he had first used, and the expenditure of strength caused him to feel noticeably weaker. The demon only blinked and returned to its attack.

Then Madoc called out a third time. The demons howled—a sound like brass trumpets blaring out of tune—and cringed still farther away. The demon bending over Randal fell back with the rest.

Master Crannach began a slow, steady chant. Randal recognized it as the reverse of Laerg's invocation—instead of calling the demon lords, Crannach was naming and dismissing them one by one. As the syllables rolled forth, two more figures came running in through the open door of the chamber: Pieter, his robes flapping around him, and Lys.

Randal's knees buckled. Pieter grabbed Randal by one arm, and Lys grabbed the other arm just as the young apprentice began to totter.

"Let's get out of here!" the junior master shouted over the uproar. "Master Madoc has to close the gate!"

Randal didn't say anything. Exhaustion and pain gripped him. He stumbled between Pieter and Lys as they pulled him out of the room and down the winding stairs. Behind them, the sound of chanting continued, mingled with demonic howlings and thunderous crashing noises.

"They'll take care of it," said Pieter, as Randal looked back over his shoulder. "Your friend in there is *good.*"

"I know," said Randal. His strength gave out then, and he sat down suddenly on the bottom step of the stairway. "He showed up just in time."

"We ran all the way," Lys told him. "Master Madoc knew something was up as soon as I told him what you told me last night, and where you were going this morning."

She nodded at Pieter. "We picked up your other friend when we got here—he was hanging around downstairs worrying because he had a feeling you were in trouble, but he didn't have the nerve to break in on somebody as high up and important as Laerg."

"Things like that never bothered Madoc," said Randal.

"You should have seen him waking up Crannach and Pullen," said Pieter with a smile. "He kicked in their doors and told them to follow, like he was talking to apprentices instead of master wizards and Regents of the Schola."

Randal leaned his head against the wall with a tired sigh. "At least I'm still alive, whatever they decide to do about me."

"What do you mean, 'whatever they decide'?" asked Lys. "Surely they won't think that you caused the mess this morning."

"Laerg's dead," said Randal. "You saw him lying there."

Lys shrugged. "After what he was doing, I don't think anybody's going to miss him very much."

"Probably not," admitted Randal. "But he died by the sword, and I'm the one who killed him."

"That *is* serious," Pieter said. "You're in deep trouble."

"What are you two talking about?" Lys asked.

"Wizards don't wear swords," Randal explained. "Or use them, except as magical symbols. No wizard has ever used a sword for a weapon, as long as anyone can remember—but I just did."

"You can't tell me you think being dead would be better," Lys said firmly. "And I don't believe your Regents will think so, either."

For the next few days, Randal held fast to that reassurance. He had a lot of time on his hands to think about it. He spent most of his waking hours packing and unpacking his few belongings, convinced at times that he would be told to leave, then hopeful that he would be allowed to stay. The wizards of the Schola were busy at work cleaning up the mess—magical and otherwise—that the demons had left behind. Nobody had much time to talk to an apprentice wizard, especially one who might well be in disgrace almost as deep as that of the fallen Laerg.

Randal's own wound was easily healed. With salves, bandages, and spells, the deep slash across his right palm mended quickly. By the time the Regents summoned him to a formal interview in the Schola library, he had only a raised, reddened scar. The skin of his palm would always be pulled tight where the sword had cut him, and if he ever had to use a knight's sword or a peasant's hoe he'd probably find the grip a painful one. For a wizard, though, the injury was minor.

The problem is, he thought glumly, as he waited outside the library door, *I don't know whether I'll still be a wizard—even an apprentice one—a few minutes from now.* He tried telling himself that it didn't matter, that he could always go back to Doun and train to be a knight like his cousin Walter, or apprentice himself to a trade as Nick had done . . . but in his heart he knew that both those ways were closed to him.

The door opened, and Randal entered the library. Once again, a group of wizards sat facing him across the long table—three of them this time: Madoc and Crannach and Mistress Pullen.

Mistress Pullen held the center seat. "Apprentice Randal," she said as he approached the table, "you have given the Regents of this Schola much to discuss."

"Discuss, indeed," said Master Crannach. "Argue to death, you mean."

Randal looked down at the floorboards. "I'm sorry."

"We don't think you meant to be a source of controversy," said Mistress Pullen. Randal thought he heard a faint note of amusement in her voice, but dismissed the idea almost at once.

"Six months ago," Pullen went on, "the examiners voted to retain you in the Schola, but on probation—and it can't be denied that since then you have made a good deal of progress. Whatever his motives may have been, Master Laerg was an excellent teacher."

"Furthermore," Crannach put in, "we have the word of the player-girl Lys that you had begun to have misgivings about Master Laerg and had been determined to find another tutor. This speaks well of your perception. And if, on that last morning, you hadn't acted to stop Laerg before his conjurings were finished, the prospects for the Schola would have been, to say the least, bleak."

"Unfortunately," said Mistress Pullen after a brief silence, "there remains the matter of the sword."

Randal clenched his fists. His right hand hurt with the movement, but he ignored it and gazed steadily at the floor. *Now's where they thank me politely and tell me I have to go.*

"The use of knightly weapons by a wizard," Pullen went on, "even by a wizard in training, is an offense against custom and tradition that we cannot let pass without imposing some kind of punishment on the offender. To kill with one disgraces the entire art."

"On the other hand," Madoc said in his deep, northerner's accent, "you didn't have much else in the way of choices . . . and you *did* act to save more lives than just your own."

"For which the Schola is not ungrateful," said Mistress Pullen. "We have accordingly arrived at a solution. It is the decision of the Regents of the Schola that you be passed out of your apprenticeship and raised to the rank of journeyman wizard."

Master Crannach smiled. "After all," he said, "the usual examination for journeyman isn't nearly as hard as what you just went through. We've never tossed an apprentice into a room full of demons, just to see what he'd do."

A wave of incredulous delight surged through Randal, but Mistress Pullen held up a hand before he could speak.

"*However,*" she said, "this decision is not a final and binding one. Your use of the sword as a weapon was dictated by necessity, but all choices have their consequences. Therefore, it is also the decision of the Regents that you be barred from any magical workings until such time as the ban is lifted."

Randal's delight went away as fast as it had come, leaving only uncertainty behind. *A wizard without magic is nothing,* he thought. *But if I'm a wizard, how can I be anything else?*

"Normally," said Madoc, "the Schola would put a binding spell on you to make sure that you comply with the ban. But I happen to believe that your sworn word is enough to hold you, and Mistress Pullen and Master Crannach have agreed to trust my

133

judgment." The northerner fixed Randal with a level, penetrating gaze. "Are you willing to give your word?"

"If you prefer," cut in Mistress Pullen, "we can employ the binding spell instead."

Randal shook his head. "I'll give my word," he said, although his voice caught in his throat as he said it. Once again, he thought that Mistress Pullen seemed to smile, this time with approval, but the expression was gone before he could be sure.

"Very well," she said. "Journeyman Randal, do you promise to refrain from all use of the magical arts whatsoever until such time as we or our chosen representative gives you permission to resume?"

He swallowed hard. To swear away his own magic . . . He'd thought that the sword-blade had hurt, but this was worse. "I so swear."

Pullen nodded. "We accept your oath. Journeyman Randal, you are dismissed."

Randal left the library. He wasn't certain what he was supposed to do next. For a while, he wandered aimlessly around the Schola buildings: the classrooms, the refectory, the dormitory with its rows of curtained rooms. Then he went to his room over the carpenter shop and started sorting out his books and clothes.

The apprentice's robe can go back to the Schola, he thought as he took off the black garment and folded it neatly. *And the books.* He looked around the small, bare room. *I don't really have much else. I can't even call my magic my own.*

He shook his head. Feeling sorry for himself

wasn't going to do any good. After a final look around the room, he went back down the stairs. Out in the street he hesitated for a moment, and then headed for the Grinning Gryphon.

Lys was singing for the midday crowd—he could hear her alto voice rising above the murmur of the patrons as he came through the door.

"Oh, you must answer my questions nine,
 Sing ninety-nine and ninety . . . "

She looked up as he came in, but didn't stop singing, although her face lit up with curiosity. Randal made his way through the crowd to his usual corner table and sat moodily contemplating a mug of cider while she finished the song.

Almost as soon as the last chords died away among the rafters, the player-girl was sliding into a seat on the bench next to him. "Well?" she asked. "Is it good or bad?"

"I don't know," he said, and told her about the Regents' decree. "So I'm a journeyman," he finished, "but I can't do magic. And I'm not really good for much else."

"You have a family," she pointed out. "You could go home."

"No," he said without stopping to think.

She looked puzzled. "Why not?"

He gave her a crooked smile. "I didn't exactly ask their permission to go off and be a wizard."

"And you think they wouldn't take you back?" she asked. "They can't be much of a family, then."

Randal thought of his uncle and his cousin Walter and all the other castle folk at Doun. "They'd take me back," he said. "But they wouldn't understand."

"So what *are* you going to do?"

He shrugged. "Make a living as best I can, I suppose. And hope someday the Regents decide to release me from my promise."

"You'll have to do more than hope, lad," said a familiar, northern-accented voice: Madoc the Wayfarer sat down on the bench across the table from Randal. "You're in for a bit of a journey, young journeyman, if you want a chance at getting your magic back."

"Where do I have to go?" asked Randal at once.

Madoc chuckled. "I told Pullen you'd jump at the chance. . . . Do you remember Master Balpesh?"

"No," admitted Randal. "Who was he?"

"Balpesh was the senior member of the Regents," said Madoc. "He presided over your admission to the Schola."

Randal remembered the old man who had told him to throw away his sword, and nodded. "I remember."

"He went off to pursue his own researches shortly afterward, and lives alone in the mountains near Tattinham," said Madoc. "The Regents have decided that if he releases you from your vow, then you will be a journeyman indeed and can practice magic as you please."

Randal felt the first stirrings of renewed hope. But Lys had been listening to the conversation with an interested expression. Now she asked, "What's the catch?"

"What makes you think there has to be one?" asked Randal.

"There always is," she said. She faced Master Madoc with a challenging expression. "Isn't there?"

The master wizard looked amused. "This time—yes. If Randal wants Balpesh's permission to work magic, he'll have to ask him in person. And Tattinham is a long way from Tarnsberg."

"Four months, at least," said Lys. "With outlaws, wild animals, bad weather, and thieving innkeepers along the way, and no magic and no weapon to help you. I remember all too well what it's like out there."

"Don't worry," said Randal, feeling a bit nettled by her worried expression. "I can manage it."

"It may be harder than you think," said Madoc. "But you don't have much choice—Balpesh hasn't left his tower since he moved in."

"Why don't you just kill him and be done with it?" Lys said to the wizard, her dark blue eyes flashing angrily. "Or do you think he really has a chance out alone like that?"

"A chance is all any of us get," said Randal.

"And you won't be going entirely unaided," Madoc told him. "I'd hate to lose you now, after all that's happened. No, I'll tell you everything I know about the route and how to find the tower, and you'll go with my finest luck spell on you."

Lys stood, tears shining on her cheeks. She looked at Randal for a moment longer. Then she picked up her lute and walked off, her shoulders set in an angry line.

Randal rose to follow her, but Madoc restrained him with a hand on his arm. "She cares about you, but you must learn to leave care behind as well. Some lessons are bitter, indeed."

The northerner drank from his own mug before continuing. "Watch yourself out there in the world, lad, and maybe you'll make it all the way to master wizard yourself someday."

Lys had taken her usual place near the center of the common room. Randal leaned back against the wall and listened as she played another of the old ballads the audiences in the Grinning Gryphon loved so well.

> "Oh, I'll ride in the foremost rank,
>   And nearest to the town,
> Because I was an earthly knight
>   They give me that renown."

The tale of true love, escape, and rescue was a long one. Lys's warm voice and the silvery ripple of the lute combined to make something as powerful, in its own way, as Madoc's images of sound and light. Randal let the music wash over him and felt at peace for the first time in months.

If I'd known three years ago what I was getting into, he thought, *I'd never have believed I'd make it this far.*

But he had made it, and could call himself a journeyman wizard with the Regents' blessing. A journeyman—and someday, perhaps, even more.

True, he still had a pilgrimage to perform before his magic was his own again, and the journeyman period itself awaited him after that—but what was a little time on the road to somebody who'd made it all the way through an apprenticeship at the School of Wizardry?